Praise for *The House of Months and Years*

"A just-scary-enough adventure that might
send readers to investigate more about real-life
'calendar houses' like Amelia's new one."
—*Kirkus Reviews*

"Amelia's loneliness and feeling of unease are striking,
thanks to Trevayne's atmospheric prose. . . . Readers will
agonize with Amelia as she weighs the cost of immortality."
—*Shelf Awareness*

"[An] engaging, well-written fantasy. A solid middle-grade
fantasy with an intriguing setting and a relatable protagonist."
—*School Library Journal*

"[Amelia's] dilemmas will resonate with readers, while the
house's Narnia-like appeal will capture their imaginations."
—*Booklist*

"[A]n eerie and enchanting story."
—*Publishers Weekly*

THE HOUSE OF
MONTHS AND YEARS

Emma Trevayne

Simon & Schuster Books for Young Readers
NEW YORK   LONDON   TORONTO   SYDNEY   NEW DELHI

SIMON & SCHUSTER BOOKS FOR YOUNG READERS
An imprint of Simon & Schuster Children's Publishing Division
1230 Avenue of the Americas, New York, New York 10020
This book is a work of fiction. Any references to historical events,
real people, or real places are used fictitiously. Other names, characters, places,
and events are products of the author's imagination, and any resemblance to
actual events or places or persons, living or dead, is entirely coincidental.
Text copyright © 2017 by Emma Trevayne
Cover illustrations copyright © 2017 by Pierre-Antoine Moelo
SIMON & SCHUSTER BOOKS FOR YOUNG READERS is a trademark of Simon &
Schuster, Inc. For information about special discounts for bulk purchases, please contact
Simon & Schuster Special Sales at 1-866-506-1949 or business@simonandschuster.com.
The Simon & Schuster Speakers Bureau can bring authors to your live event. For more
information or to book an event, contact the Simon & Schuster Speakers Bureau
at 1-866-248-3049 or visit our website at www.simonspeakers.com.
Also available in a Simon & Schuster Books for Young Readers hardcover edition
Cover design by Lizzy Bromley
Interior design by Hilary Zarycky
The text for this book was set in ITC New Baskerville.
Manufactured in the United States of America
0318 OFF
First Simon & Schuster Books for Young Readers paperback edition April 2018
2 4 6 8 10 9 7 5 3 1
The Library of Congress has cataloged the hardcover edition as follows:
Names: Trevayne, Emma, author.
Title: The house of months and years / Emma Trevayne.
Description: First edition. | New York : Simon & Schuster Books for Young Readers,
[2017] | Summary: "A girl must stop the Boogeyman living in her home from stealing
her family's warmest memories"—Provided by publisher.
Identifiers: LCCN 2016013886 | ISBN 9781481462556 (hardback) |
ISBN 9781481462570 (eBook)
Subjects: | CYAC: Dwellings—Fiction. | Memory—Fiction. | Adventure and
Adventurers—Fiction. | BISAC: JUVENILE FICTION / Fantasy & Magic. |
JUVENILE FICTION / Action & Adventure / General. | JUVENILE FICTION /
Mysteries & Detective Stories.
Classification: LCC PZ7.T73264 Ho 2017 | DDC [Fic]—dc23
LC record available at https://lccn.loc.gov/2016013886
ISBN 9781481462563 (pbk)

For Zareen
and
for Tony,
who, in different ways, brought this house to life

ACKNOWLEDGMENTS

When I first heard of calendar houses several years ago, the idea immediately gripped me. How could such a thing not make its way into the pages of a book? It took some time to settle on the story and its characters, but once I did, Amelia, Horatio, and Nudiustertian House became as real to me as the room in which I wrote about them. No book, though, is written in complete isolation, no matter how alluring the image of a lone writer at her keyboard. For their help and support in both tangible and intangible ways, I would like to mention the following people:

My family, of course, who did everything from listen to me rant about time travel to drawing up blueprints for an imaginary house so I'd stop losing track of Amelia and her family in all the rooms.

Zareen Jaffery, who understood Amelia from the start, and who has understood me from the start, too. Also everyone at Simon & Schuster BFYR, especially Lizzy Bromley, Hilary Zarycky, and Mekisha Telfer.

Pierre-Antoine Moelo, who illustrated the beautiful cover.

So many friends who helped with plot tangles, met

up with me for writing dates, and sent me hilarious texts while reading early drafts—Claire Legrand, Heidi Schulz, and Tom Pollock chief among them. Stefan Bachmann gets bonus points for reading and mailing me Swiss chocolate.

Amy Plum, for organizing a writing retreat in an old, crumbling, haunted(!) building in the French country-side. I arrived armed with little more than the proposed idea and left with thousands of words steeped, I hope, in atmosphere.

Brooks Sherman and the Bent Agency, for all their hard work.

All of the readers of my previous books who got in touch while I was writing this one to say they were excited to see something new. When you sit down at your computer and stare at a blank page, afraid the words won't come, there is no better boost than the arrival of a note from someone who really wants you to keep going.

Thank you.

The important thing about having lots of things to remember is that you've got to go somewhere afterward where you can remember them, you see? You've got to stop. You haven't really been anywhere until you've got back home.

—TERRY PRATCHETT, *The Light Fantastic*

THE HOUSE OF
MONTHS AND YEARS

PROLOGUE

A SHADOW MOVED THROUGH AN empty house, a deeper smudge of darkness in the gloom of unlit rooms. Many rooms, but not countless ones. The number was important. Details were important, and there were as many details as there were grains of dust on the mantelpieces or seconds of silence in the night. Or raindrops, whispering against the windows from the last of the bitter winter storms.

Icicles hung like fingernails from the pipes in the cellar, the heat running through them as fast as it could to escape upward. They would not melt, not ever. Other shadows lurked there, ordinary ones, the strange shapes caused by objects abandoned when the last residents had left. The shadow hadn't wanted them to leave. It trembled and slipped up the stairs. The ground floor was only cool, the conservatory keeping a secret of spring that it would soon tell. In the kitchen the pantry was empty, the oven the coldest thing in the room. Nobody ate in the kitchen, or read in the library, or relaxed in the sitting room.

Up more stairs, nobody dreamed in the bedrooms. The shadow shimmered and melted in the warmth of them, almost stifling, as it moved from one to the next. Soon, soon the rooms would have beds, and the beds people. Soon someone would come and dust the mantelpieces, clear the junk in the cellar, make the house *their* home, one they wanted to live in.

The shadow oozed its way up one final corkscrew to the attic, slid across bare floorboards to a curiously shaped window.

Trees surrounded the house in every direction, the forest sliced in two by a long driveway, which led to a road, which led to a town, which led to a city, which led to the rest of the world.

That was one way to get there.

There were others.

The house shivered and groaned beneath the shadow. It had been empty much too long. Far below the window, a sign swung from a wooden post, lashed, thrashed by the storm.

The shadow grinned, and by the flash from a bolt of lightning, a man stepped from where the shadow had just been. His suit was old, musty, creased, his hair wild. It was time for him to leave—temporarily, of course. He would return soon, but for now it wouldn't do to be late to supper. He brushed his lapels and descended the stairs as noiselessly as he had come, glided past the empty bedrooms, slid away from the clatter of rain on the conservatory's windows, slipped out the front door and under the swinging sign.

SOLD, it read.

The man smiled his way down the long drive and became a shadow once more.

CHAPTER ONE

A House but Not a Home

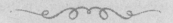

THE HOUSE KNEW. IT KNEW, gazing down at her with its droopy window-eyes, that Amelia hated it. It knew with its wide, crumbling, scowling face that she was scowling right back at it, and she had a tongue she could stick out, which she did, as far as it would go. She was better than the house. It might be big and old and in the middle of a forest, but she was still better. She didn't only have a tongue; she had shoes for kicking at the driveway and a big dictionary full of insulting words she could hurl at the bricks.

Really, her glower had little to do with the house, which Amelia had to admit looked interesting—and in her opinion *interesting* was far more of a compliment than *nice.* Deep down, she knew it wasn't the windows or the wood or the slate tiles on the roof. She didn't want to be there, but it was more, just, well, all of it, and she would get in trouble for sticking her tongue out at her cousins. Especially since another thing she knew deep down was that this whole situation wasn't her cousins' fault. What had happened was very sad, and Amelia felt very sad *for* them, but she could be just as sad in her own room, in her own house.

So this one, in front of her, was a safer target for her annoyance.

You don't like me now, little girl, but you will learn to. Come inside, the house seemed to say. In her imagination the house sounded like a wheezy, whispering old man. Amelia stretched her tongue out as far as it would go.

"You'll freeze that way," said her mother, dragging a bursting suitcase from the car. It had dents in the side from where Amelia had been wedged against it for the whole of the long journey.

Good, thought Amelia, though her mother was wrong. It was much too warm here for anything to freeze. The latticework of leaves surrounding them was lush and green, the trees holding the heat in cupped wooden hands. A month from now, perhaps, the edges of the leaves would begin to turn gold. Two months and they'd cover the ground on which Amelia Howling stood.

She didn't want to be here that long. It had already been too long.

She wanted to go home.

Voices came through the open door. Quiet voices. The accident had turned down the volume on Amelia's life. The ringing phone had been the last loud noise, the call that made her mother go silent and pale. It wasn't surprising that the silence had fallen here, too. It had started here. Or, to be precise, it had started on the road leading to the town, on a night booming with thunder and crackling with lightning and slick with sheets of rain. A scream of twisting metal, and then a hush that had spread all the way to Amelia's house.

An old, curly-haired woman stepped out onto the porch, wiping her hands on a cloth before waving at Amelia and her parents. Amelia did not wave back, but Mrs. Howling did. Mrs. Howling had dropped the phone after that awful call and rushed here, stayed here while Amelia finished school and Mr. Howling packed boxes every evening after work. The old woman, a housekeeper of some sort, had agreed to look after Amelia's cousins these past few days while

Mrs. Howling returned to help with the last bits and pieces.

Amelia ran up the steps and darted past the woman into the entrance hall. A rack there still held coats too large to belong to her cousins, too small for the house-keeper, and none of them were her mother's. Amelia tiptoed across the floor to peer into the sitting room, ignoring the conversation that started behind her.

"Hello," said her eldest cousin, Owen. He was ten, just a week older than Amelia herself, and that made her angry. It had never bothered her before, when she'd seen him at Christmases or family holidays, but a lot of things were different now. This house was different; they'd lived somewhere else the last time she'd visited. *Owen* was different. It had in fact been a few years since she'd seen him; his hair was darker than it had been, darker than hers, and he had more freckles than she remembered. Perhaps he'd always had that many.

"Hello," answered Amelia, so late it seemed Owen had forgotten he'd said it first. He'd gone back to some silly game on the gadget in his lap. She had one too, and was probably better at the game than he was.

The other two, Matthew and Lavender, were younger. Eight and one. More than once Amelia had overheard her father say that Lavender, at least, probably didn't grasp what had happened. Matthew was staring at a spot on the ugly striped wallpaper, and Lavender wore a smile frosted with crumbs.

Amelia *did* understand what had happened. She was plenty old enough, thank you very much, even if she wasn't oldest anymore. That was the most excellent thing about being an only child: She got to be the oldest and the youngest, all at the same time. She understood that her aunt and uncle had died, and now her parents had to be Owen, Matthew, and Lavender's parents too.

Not that they ever would be, of course, not truly. Amelia knew *someone* had to care for them—she wasn't stupid—but she didn't understand why it needed to be like this. She'd offered to share her room at home, but apparently that house still wasn't big enough for everyone. She'd suggested that the old woman could look after them all the time, and Amelia and her parents would just visit, but that wasn't all right either. The woman wasn't even staying. She was only ever meant to be temporary, and wanted to retire. Mrs. Howling said she'd clean the house herself—with help from Amelia's father and the children, of course. It figured that no matter how far she moved, Amelia couldn't escape chores.

"We're sorry, Amie; we know it's a big change," her father had said, taping up a cardboard box in her old living room.

"We really don't have the space there, but this house is very large," her mother had said on the phone when she'd called to wish Amelia good night. "It only makes sense. Besides, they've already been through so much. We can't take their home from them too."

But it was perfectly fine to take Amelia's home. Her perfect little house on its perfect little hill, with her very best friend right next door, and the pond at the bottom of the garden, and Mrs. Frenkel at school to give her interesting books.

Oh, yes. It was *fine* to take all that away.

Beyond the sitting room a conservatory filled with underwater light and wicker furniture spread the fresh scent of plants and flowers. And there was Mum's computer, set up on a little table so she could do her work. Amelia paid no attention to Owen following her as she wandered through the glass room, into a kitchen that took up most of the back of the house. A plate of cakes sat on the enormous table, which explained Lavender's mess. Through the windows Amelia saw a large garden, bright with even more plants and flowers and, past them, more of the trees that encircled the whole place.

Owen was still watching her, and it was too much. She opened her mouth, but nothing came out. She felt so very sorry for him and just couldn't find words for it under all the sorry she felt for herself, so it was better to say nothing at all. She ran back the way she'd come, past her parents still talking to the housekeeper in the doorway and up the wide, curved stairs that creaked like an old man's bones under her. The first thing she felt when she reached the top was stifling heat, and the first thing she saw was a closed door, and being on the other side of it seemed like a very good idea.

"You can't go in there," said Owen as she reached for the knob. "You're not allowed."

Amelia stopped, turned to face him. "Is that your room?"

Owen shook his head. "No. It's where my dad does his work."

Not anymore, thought Amelia, but it was a sad thought, not a mean one.

"Then you can't tell me what to do," she said.

"That's yours," he answered, pointing at the room beside the office and backing away, descending the stairs again. Someone—the old woman, surely, because Mrs. Howling knew Amelia better than this— had made an effort to decorate Amelia's room in a way that would surely be described as *jolly*, and anything described that way is the exact opposite, always. Little wooden letters, each a different color, spelled out her name on the door.

If Amelia were to be sick on the rug after eating too many sweets, it would be in precisely those colors.

It was tempting to do so. In fact, she did feel slightly ill. It was too warm up here, far warmer than even the summer day outside should allow for.

And being sick might distract her parents from bringing the suitcases into the house.

Instead she swallowed and stepped inside the room. It wasn't a bad room. Not as nice as her old one, obviously, but it was larger, with a big bay window and its own fireplace. Since it was summer, the hearth was dark, full of sooty shadows that stole what light they could from the rest of the room.

It had a window seat, too, and someone—this time it probably *had* been Mrs. Howling—had piled one end high with books. Amelia's own books, sent ahead in the boxes her father had packed in a big van.

Well. They wouldn't get her to like it here that easily.

You will like it here, insisted the room, the fireplace, the surrounding forest. *You will.*

A gust of wind blew from somewhere, rattling her

windows, slamming her door. Downstairs, suitcases crashed and bumped into the front hall. Amelia wondered if maybe she should help, if only so as not to get in trouble later, but her cousins weren't helping either, far as she could hear with the door closed, so that settled that.

The bed was comfortable, which was deeply irritating. Complaining that it was lumpy, that she wouldn't sleep a wink on it, that she missed her old one . . . that would feel like *something*. A protest against the strange, welcoming feeling tickling at the back of Amelia's neck. The house *wanted* people in it, and even inside her own head that sounded an odd way to put it, but she could think of no other description. The long driveway had drawn them in, through the two wide swathes of trees, to shelter them inside the clearing that held the house.

Shelter. That was the word. Amelia's large dictionary wasn't one of the books on the window seat—she'd insisted on keeping it with her, and it was still in the car—but she knew if she checked it, she'd be right. *Shelter* was definitely the proper word. Beyond the trees there were roads and cars and cities and life, creeping up to the edge of the house's surrounding land but not daring to infringe upon it. It was so quiet, the house, so proud. It stood tall in its own gardens and didn't need any other houses around it to tell it what it was.

Well. Amelia could tell what it wasn't. It wasn't home, and it never would be.

A clock ticked on Amelia's nightstand, but its rhythmic noise wasn't what had woken her. She didn't know what had, until Lavender let loose another screeching wail, which was quickly followed by the sound of Mrs. Howling trying to comfort her. This had happened every night of the two weeks since Amelia arrived, and now she was too annoyed to simply roll over and fall back to sleep.

It was twelve minutes to midnight, a pleasing symmetry, and Amelia had kicked off all her covers, the room still too warm. She felt as if she'd been asleep for only a second, though her father had come in almost three hours before to kiss her good night and turn off the lamp. He'd tried to close the curtains, too, but she'd stopped him, and now the moon shone into the clearing, into Amelia's room. It chilled the floor with its cold, white light, bleaching the floorboards to more bones that groaned; if the stairs were the house's spine, these were its ribs.

The hairs on the back of Amelia's neck rose. The

window seemed even more like an eye from inside than it had when she first saw the house. It stared out through the gaps in the trees to spy on the rooftops of the town. Amelia hadn't been to the town yet; all she knew of it was what she'd seen when they drove through on their way here, and she'd been too squashed in with the suitcases to pay much attention. The suitcases were empty now, tossed down into the cellar.

She was really staying here.

For fourteen days she'd been trapped in this place. Most of the time had been spent reading on her window seat and avoiding her cousins, though her parents had some very firm rules about mealtimes, especially supper. Three times a day, she slunk sullenly to the kitchen and ate in silence while her mum's lips got thinner and thinner and her dad's fork clanged too heavily against his plate. When she was finished, she would disappear back to her room, and at some point one of her parents would come to tuck her into bed, saying little except they hoped she'd sleep well.

Now she was wide awake, kneeling on the window seat, looking out at the trees. The leaves and the spaces between them played with the dark of the night and the light of the moon, making shapes and faces. An eye winked at her and rustled back on the wind to ordinary treeness. Lavender had stopped crying, and a hush, a real hush, which is a special kind of silence, fell over the house once more. It was disturbed only by the ticktock on the nightstand, the hands neatly sweeping away every last speck of Amelia's old life.

It was just . . . it was just *silly* that it could be quite so simple. That everything she'd known could vanish so easily and leave her with nothing but memories. Silly and wrong.

Her bedroom was still too hot; her throat stuck to itself. The house was quiet, and carefully, so as not to start Lavender's cacophony up again, Amelia crept to her door and opened it, tiptoeing past the sickly colored letters and down the stairs for a glass of water. Voices came from the kitchen, her mother and father talking. Amelia inched up to the door and peered inside. Mrs. Howling had Lavender balanced on one hip.

"She needs time," said Mr. Howling, messing up his usually very neat hair with his hand.

Lavender needed time to go back to sleep? Amelia couldn't remember being only a year old. Maybe she'd been the same way.

"I know," replied Mrs. Howling, "but this isn't making the situation any easier. I've tried to talk to her, even offered to take her shopping for some new books, just the two of us, but she's having none of it. I think she's still angry with me for leaving the two of you and coming here, but what choice was there?"

Amelia's heart skipped. They weren't talking about Lavender; they were talking about *her*. How dare they talk about her behind her back, but that was what parents did, wasn't it? And it was true she'd told Mum she didn't want to go to the bookshop.

It was true that she was still angry, too.

"There wasn't a choice," said her father, kissing her mother's cheek. Ew. "Of course you had to come look after these three, and Hugo and Marie would have done the same for Amelia, if something had happened to us. We're all adjusting. A new house, more kids around, my new job. We'll make it work, darling."

Amelia slipped back upstairs, thirsty and thinking. She hated it here, but at least she still had her parents. Her cousins must feel much worse. She *could* try harder to be friends with them. A few days earlier, Amelia had overheard Matthew telling Owen he wanted their mum and dad back.

Well, Amelia wanted them to have their mum and dad back too.

She was overhearing quite a lot these days, but it

wasn't her fault. The house was so big and wonky it was impossible not to find herself in a forgotten room or around a corner, on the few occasions she left her window seat. And if she pressed herself a little deeper into the shadows and strain her ears, as she'd done at the kitchen door, well, that was just a very sensible mistake.

There was nothing to overhear now. The hush had fallen once more. The clock ticked and a new noise joined it: a branch tapping at the window. Good grief, how did anyone ever sleep here, where even the silences were loud? And where the trees cast tall, creepy shadows on the walls like skeleton giants, waving their arms around their heads?

She got into bed and closed her eyes. She was going to sleep, and she was going to dream of something pleasant. That time she and her very best friend, Isabelle, had found that cave by the seaside, perhaps, or last Christmas, when Mum and Dad had given her the dictionary she'd wanted, after asking her at least a dozen times beforehand if she was certain.

Of course she'd been certain. Or, according to the thing itself, she'd *coveted* the dictionary. It was thick enough to make a convenient step when she needed something too. Amelia liked things that were good for more than one job.

She may have dreamed of sand or pine needles, roaring oceans, or glittering, multicolored baubles. She may have dreamed about the time she and her parents had gone on holiday to the desert and ridden actual camels, but when she awoke in the morning she couldn't quite remember dreaming anything, which was strange, but not. At home Amelia had always remembered her dreams and told her mother about them over breakfast, but here, in the comfortable bed in the too-warm room, they disappeared the moment she opened her eyes. Maybe she would've remembered if Owen hadn't knocked on her door, startling her from sleep. He didn't even wait for an answer before barging in as if he owned the place. It might be his house, and quite frankly he could keep it, but this was her room.

Yes, it is your room, and you should protect what is yours, the room whispered inside her head, gathering itself around her. The voice chased away any sympathetic thoughts she'd had in the middle of the night.

"What do you want?" she asked.

"I was only wondering if you wanted to come outside with me and Matthew. There's a frog."

"There were tons of frogs in the pond at my old house. A million frogs. Frogs are boring."

"Suit yourself, then."

"And stay out of my room. I know you've been in here. Yesterday my dictionary was under my bed, and *I* didn't put it there."

He glared at her—an admission of guilt if she'd ever seen one—and shut the door harder than was strictly necessary. She would suit herself. She'd suit herself right after breakfast.

"Good morning, sweetheart," said her mother. "You slept late; are you feeling well?"

"Yes. My room is still too hot, though," answered Amelia, taking her seat at the long wooden table and looking at the half-empty butter dish, the bottle of syrup with a sticky drip running down its side. "Are there pancakes?" By daylight, with just her and Mum in the kitchen, it was easy to push aside her anger, and pancakes buy a lot of forgiveness.

"We'll get you a fan or something. Ours is warm too, and the basement is freezing. We'll get someone in to look at the heating soon. Old houses can be so odd. There were pancakes," said her mother, frowning. "We didn't have as much milk as I thought; I'm not used to shopping for six."

So there were no pancakes, and it wasn't even just her and Mum in the kitchen. A grubby-faced Lavender peeked out from behind a cupboard, fist full of soggy mush that Amelia was sure had once been *her* breakfast.

"How about toast?" asked her mother.

"I'm not hungry," said Amelia. Her stomach growled under the table, loud as a begging dog.

"Oh, Amie, I am sorry." Mrs. Howling put two slices of bread in the toaster anyway. "I'll make whatever you like for dinner." But Amelia was already out of the kitchen and, because it was the closest door, clomping down the basement stairs.

She hadn't been down here yet. It had taken her the first week to learn how not to get lost in the rooms aboveground, if only so she could get lost on purpose, otherwise known as hiding. The basement had seemed too obvious a place to hide, and the discovery of a library near the kitchen had rather answered the question for her, on the occasions she'd wanted to leave her room.

Mum was right; it was freezing down here. Pipes, white with filigreed frost, ran along the walls, and huge icicles hung from the seams where one joined another.

Something rustled in a corner. She whirled around. "Hello? Owen? Matthew?"

No answer came, and she didn't think they'd be lurking to scare her on the off chance she'd decided to come down here. Probably a mouse, though why it wouldn't choose to live upstairs in the warmth was beyond her. Mum should keep the ice cream down here—if her cousins hadn't already eaten it all—next to the assorted junk that always gathers in basements. This one was no exception: rusted bicycle frames and tins of paint on rickety shelves too ugly to be on display in the rest of the house. Atop an old, shabby dresser sat a broken Christmas bauble, a grubby tobacco pipe, a single child's shoe. There were boxes, too, but they hadn't come with Amelia and her parents in the car, or in the hired moving van that had made the journey ahead of them.

Owen, Matthew, and Lavender had only lived here since February, and it was just the beginning of August now. It looked as if their parents hadn't even had a chance to fully unpack before the accident. She peered into the top of a box that turned out to hold winter coats, unused since they'd arrived. It simply didn't make sense that Amelia had to live here; it wasn't as if her cousins had grown up here or anything, not like she had in her house.

Another box held old photographs. Someone should move them upstairs; they were being damaged by the cold. Half the ones she could see had turned a pale gray, with only the faintest outlines of their original subjects showing. She'd tell Mum later, if she remembered.

It was too cold to stay here. Whatever the basement seemed to think, it was summer outside, and she was only wearing a T-shirt and shorts.

Whatever the basement seemed to think. That was a curious way to phrase it, but it felt like the right way. The right words, and a girl with Amelia's dictionary would know. That was it.

Since the moment she'd arrived, the house had given her the feeling it could think for itself.

CHAPTER TWO

Pasts & Presences

THE FEELING DID NOT GO away. Amelia checked her dictionary. The feeling did not *dissipate*. That was a good word, one she'd temporarily forgotten, though she was struggling with some of the others. If her mother or father decided to ask, she'd have difficulty describing exactly what it was about the house that gave her such a strange tingle at the back of her neck, the sensation of constantly being watched. She'd duck into the nearest room to hide at the sound of Owen or Matthew's approaching footsteps and have to check that Lavender wasn't hiding behind the furniture, so sure was Amelia that she wasn't alone.

But Mum and Dad wouldn't ask; they were too busy.

And even if Amelia could answer, they'd surely tell her it was just because she wasn't used to the house yet. Which was true, but irrelevant. The house was weird.

"Mum, there's some pictures in the basement that are getting ruined by the cold," Amelia said that night at dinner, pleased with herself for remembering something that wasn't a word.

"Oh, thank you, Amie. I'll try to find the time to move them tomorrow."

Amelia's father finished chewing a bite of spaghetti, which was not the "whatever you like" Amelia had been promised to replace the missed pancakes. If she'd wanted to eat worms, she'd have eaten actual worms. She had, once, dared by the now-faraway Isabelle. "I'll double your pocket money for the month if you help out your mum by moving them to the attic," he said. "You could buy a thesaurus."

He said it with a smile, but it was not, in fact, a terrible idea. Neither was annoying Owen across the table. His mouth was open, still full of food, and she could just *tell* he was about to take the offer instead. Owen probably didn't want a thesaurus, but his eyes were glinting at the thought of extra pocket money.

"Will you take me to a bookshop?" she asked.

"On Sunday," said her father.

"All right, then."

Owen's freckles bunched together as he scowled, then filled his mouth with another whole plateful of spaghetti, because boys were disgusting. Amelia grinned. Ha.

"I'd get something better than a poxy book," he said later, trailing her up the stairs at bedtime. "A new game, or flashing lights for my bike, or—"

"Good thing I'm not you, then, isn't it?" A new video game would have been Amelia's second choice for her newfound riches, but she wasn't going to give him the satisfaction. At least he wouldn't want to borrow her thesaurus. "I want a book. You probably can't even read."

"Hey! I can too."

"Sorry," she said, not really meaning it.

"There's a library full of books downstairs, seeing as you seem to like 'em more than people."

"More than *some* people. And I know." Aunt Marie and Uncle Hugo, Owen's parents, hadn't found time to unpack their photographs after moving here, but they'd put thousands of volumes carefully on their shelves. That made Amelia like them, even if she hadn't known them very well. Every other Christmas and a handful of summer afternoons weren't really enough to get to know people, but clearly they'd had their priorities in order. "Why did you move here?" she asked, annoyed with herself for letting the question slip out. It didn't much matter why they'd moved here; what mattered was that she'd had to.

But she did want to know why anyone would choose a huge, rambling, crumbling old house in the middle of nowhere, with only a sleepy little town nearby pretending it was a real place people wanted to be.

"Dunno." Owen shrugged. "They didn't really tell us. I just remember them being all excited about how special it was; apparently houses like this are hardly ever for sale. Because they've all fallen down already, I expect."

"You don't like it? Do you think it's creepy too?"

He shrugged again. "It's a house. It's all right. I miss my friends from where we used to live. Least your parents let you wait and finish school; I had to switch right in the middle, and I didn't know anyone. Mum and Dad loved this house, though, the moment they saw it. Wanted to move in right away." His eyes turned sad, and Amelia remembered.

"I'm sorry," she said.

"Thank you. D'you know, these are the most words you've said to me since you got here? Hey, remember the time I got that remote-control car, and we drove it in the snow and it got stuck?"

"That's not true," said Amelia to the first part, but she knew it was. All of it was true. They *had* wedged the car into a snowdrift, and Izzy, her best friend, had dug it out with her hands, and Mum had needed to dry the insides with her hair dryer before it would go again. She considered adding more words, another question, but he might get the foolish idea they were friends or something, and she wasn't entirely sure she wanted to hear that he thought the house was watching him too. Or worse, he'd laugh at her. "Good night," she said instead, running for her room and shutting the door behind her.

She stubbed her toe on a box. Mum hadn't nagged her to unpack them yet, had only looked pointedly at the stack every time she'd come to tuck Amelia in or put away clean socks. Unpacking, finding a home for each of the treasures inside, meant something. It meant they were truly staying.

Perhaps one box wouldn't hurt. Just the one she'd kicked, mind you. The house was full of things that belonged to everyone else, and as the voice in her head had reminded her that morning, this was her room. Even if it wasn't as good as her old one.

The box contained everything that had been on Amelia's dresser back home: a snow globe from a holiday; a miniature rocking horse won at a fair; a photograph, protected by a silver frame, of her and Isabelle on their first day of school; a fancy hairbrush Amelia had never used on her very ordinary hair. It had once belonged to her grandmother.

She set each object carefully in its place on her new dresser. They didn't look the same here; the color of the wood was all wrong. It would have to do.

The door opened behind her. "Oh, that's nice," said her father. "I'm glad you're getting settled."

"May I write Isabelle a letter?" Amelia asked, looking at the picture.

"Of course." Mr. Howling was a tall man, and he had to lean down to peer inside the frame. "You miss her, don't you?"

Amelia didn't answer.

"I know it doesn't feel like it now, but you'll make new friends here, Amie. There's Owen, of course, and it will be even easier when school starts. Still, it's always good to keep in touch with the old ones. Do you want to use my computer?"

"Real letters are better," said Amelia, shaking her head.

"You know, I agree with you. You write the letter; I'll

put a stamp on it and post it on my way to work."

"Thanks, Dad."

An eardrum-piercing shriek came from across the hall. Lavender wasn't a Howling—she had a different last name—but she *was* howling. Amelia's father grimaced. "I'd better go help with that," he said. "Goodness, it's been a long time since we had such a young child."

Amelia frowned. "She's not your daughter."

"Oh, Amie, you're our daughter, but Lavender, and Matthew and Owen, are family as well. We all have to be one big family now." He kissed the top of her head and left her to change into her pajamas. Amelia put the photograph in the bottom of the drawer and got into bed without brushing her teeth.

Nobody noticed.

They didn't notice that she stayed awake far too late either, hiding under the covers with a flashlight she'd dug from one of the remaining boxes, bright like a sun in the night of the little tent she'd made. Her pencil scratched like the whispered conversations she and Isabelle used to have on nights just like this one, with a breeze blowing outside and no school to worry about in the morning. She told Izzy about the stupid house and the stupid feeling it gave her, and her stupid cousins, and the thesaurus she was going to get with her extra pocket money. She asked how the pond at the bottom of the garden was doing, technically on Amelia's side, but there was no fence, so it had just been one big place for them to run around.

She was so tired by the time she finally switched off the light that she didn't notice the tree casting its long, thin shadow on her wall, that of a man waving wild arms around wild hair. And she was still so sleepy when Mum woke her for breakfast that she didn't look in the drawer when she grabbed her socks, or at anything much, really.

It would be some time before she'd dig to the bottom of that drawer again, by which time it would be too late. She'd know exactly why the photograph in its silver frame had turned a pale, ghostly gray.

For now, however, she did not know, and was sure that by lugging the boxes from the freezing basement to the much warmer attic, she was saving the contents from any further damage.

And earning herself a thesaurus.

It was actually rather nice up here. Cooler than Amelia's sweltering bedroom, with a scent in the air that tickled the edges of memory with fingertips of recollection. She sniffed deeply and was transported to last November and the bonfire they'd had in the garden of her old house. They'd built a huge one, her and Mum and Dad, and Isabelle and Isabelle's parents. They'd roasted marshmallows on long sticks.

The attic smelled of burning leaves. It was too early in the year for anyone to be starting a fire outside; the trees surrounding the house were all too green. Amelia thought she'd read somewhere that smells could trigger the strongest memories, and, closing her eyes, she was right back in her old garden, watching sparks dance and pop in the air.

She wished this room could be her bedroom, but Mum and Dad would never allow it. She already knew what they'd say: that it wouldn't be fair to the others. As if living here at all was fair to Amelia. She liked the walls of worn red brick, the bare boards that creaked as she carried the boxes of photographs one by one to an empty corner. Most of the attic was empty. Sunlight streamed in through an oddly shaped window, making strange patterns on the floor.

The light wasn't the only unusual thing. Someone had made markings below the windows in blue chalk. Amelia went for a closer look, careful not to smudge them with her socks.

Smudging might have made them easier to read. As it was, she could find no sense in the illegible scribbles. That was a 5, maybe? And that a two? She couldn't be sure, even without the added complication of not knowing what the numbers would mean if she was right.

It was probably just Matthew, anyway. She'd seen him outside, scribbling on the paved portion of the driveway with chalks of all different colors, including blue.

The silence up here was lovely, another proper hush. She couldn't hear Lavender crying or babbling, depending on what moment of the day it was. She couldn't hear Owen shouting at his video game or Matthew begging to be allowed a turn. Amelia had noticed that Owen always gave in, in the end, handing over the game just when Matthew's frown got a little too deep.

She sat in the corner next to the boxes, savoring the quiet, and looked again in the top of the nearest. The undamaged pictures all showed her aunt, uncle, and cousins looking happy on holidays or at the home they'd lived in before this one. Amelia recognized the living room, a Christmas tree, one of her own old socks on a foot sneaking into the edge of the photograph.

It was a bit sad, really. Not the accident, which was

very sad, of course, but that Amelia hadn't known them better. She'd always left them talking to her parents and played with Owen, or by herself, because grown-ups were boring, especially when you got a bunch of them together. Judging from the books in the library, they'd been very interested in history, but she didn't know what they had done for jobs or for fun.

These thoughts only made Amelia feel more alone. She could ask anyone in the house and they'd know more than she did, except for Lavender, and that was only because she was too young. On all the floors below, her parents and cousins were getting on with the business of trying to be one big family and didn't need Amelia's help.

A shadow slid over the wall and across Amelia's toes, which suddenly felt very cold. She kept seeing them, tall, thin shadows with profiles of grinning faces. The photograph in her hand was pulled from her fingers— or had she simply dropped it? She jumped and ran to the window, where the sun was high in the sky and no trees stood near enough.

A shiver ran through Amelia like the beginning of a terrible flu. She fled across the attic and down the stairs as fast as she could, past the sound of yelling and a slamming door, into the kitchen. Mum raised her head from her hands, elbows on the countertop.

"This house is haunted," said Amelia. It was perfectly clear to her now. The house had read her mind when she first arrived, and put the welcoming voice in her head, and everywhere she looked she saw shadows shaped like people. She'd read ghost stories before. It was obvious. Haunted houses were always old and crumbling and weird.

Mrs. Howling's face dropped back down, and when her voice came, it was muffled. "Enough, Amelia. I know you don't like it here, but I won't have you making up stories to try to get us to leave. You aren't the only one having a difficult time. What with you making it clear this isn't your home, and Owen reminding me I'm not his mum . . ."

Mrs. Howling was crying. Amelia could hear the tears, though she couldn't see them.

"Well, that's all true . . . ," Amelia began. It was precisely the wrong thing to say, even if she hadn't meant it quite the way it had sounded.

"Go to your room, Amelia, now. And don't come out until you're ready to be helpful."

Irritation sparked all through Amelia's bones like the bonfire she'd been remembering, five seconds from blazing. She stomped from the kitchen. She *had* been helpful. She'd taken the boxes to the attic, hadn't she? And been roundly frightened as a result, though anger was doing a fine job of chasing the fear away. What was the point of being helpful if no one noticed? Pointing out this creepy house was haunted was pretty helpful too, in Amelia's opinion, but nobody wanted to listen.

She didn't go to her room. Let them find her and punish her if they cared to. Books had always listened, always understood her. Thousands—all right, probably only hundreds, but a lot—lined the walls of the library. They swallowed all the noise from outside and, soon, all of Amelia's annoyance and lingering traces of fear.

It was difficult to hate anyone who'd owned this many books, and she didn't truly hate her aunt and uncle. The accident hadn't been their fault. It was an odd sort of joke, that the people she currently liked most in the house were the lingering ghosts of those who didn't live in it anymore.

Ghosts. Amelia startled. Was that who she'd seen in the attic? She couldn't say why, but it had felt like a man. Her uncle? Was that the feeling the house gave her?

She turned her head to the side and moved slowly down the walls of shelves, reading the spines. They must have had something . . .

Aha. A whole section, just like in a proper library.

She pulled out one of the books, chosen because it was the thickest and oldest-looking. *Ancient Spirits of the Islands.* Its spine was cracked nearly in two, its pages thin as winter skin.

Aside from the books, the best part of the library was the furniture. Amelia curled up in an armchair so red and soft she might have been inside one of the roses in the conservatory. Her fright was entirely gone now; this room was too comforting for anything to bother her here. She was safe here.

She began to read.

The book wasn't only about ghosts. All manner of monsters, spirits, fairies, sprites, and general creatures with wings jumped out from the paper, but none of them caught Amelia's eye as the thing she'd seen. None of their descriptions captured the feeling she got from the house. So either it wasn't there or the author had gotten it wrong.

Or she was imagining things.

Which was possible, she supposed. Mum had accused her of making up stories, and she wasn't, but her mind could be tricking her. The thing about imagining, though, was that she usually knew she was doing it. She and Isabelle used to come up with all kinds of mad stories, or pretend an old sled in the garage was really a spaceship, but they'd always known it was only pretend.

They had once . . .

Amelia frowned. They'd once . . . It had been on the first day of school; they'd done something. . . . Her brain was too full of the book in her lap to remember exactly what. But it had been fun.

"Amie?"

Amelia slammed the book, tummy hot with a rush of guilt. She was supposed to be in her room, but her mother smiled a bit as she came into the library, closing the door behind her.

"I'm sorry I snapped at you, darling. I do know this is difficult for you, and you're doing the best you can. Just try to remember it isn't easy on any of us, all right?"

"I'll try," said Amelia, deciding not to repeat what she'd said earlier. Mum might not take it any better a second time. Besides, everyone else in the house got to know things she didn't. Why shouldn't she have a secret too?

"Thank you," said Mrs. Howling, gazing around the room. "They loved books, like you do." Tears filled her eyes again. "Put them back when you're done?"

"I will."

"Good girl." Mrs. Howling slipped from the room, leaving Amelia alone with the heavy tome on her lap. *Tome* was her favorite word for "book," but the answers she needed weren't in this one. She went back to the section where she'd found it, looking up and down the shelves. A promising one sat high up, far over Amelia's head, beyond her reach even if she stood on tiptoe.

Huffing, she dragged the nearest chair over to the shelves, shifting it an inch at a time. Even standing on the seat didn't get her as high up as she needed.

Very carefully, she placed her knee on the back of the chair and hoisted herself up, fingertips gripping the edge of a shelf to keep her balance. She hadn't moved the chair close enough, but she could reach if she leaned forward. . . .

Her stomach flipped over the instant the chair began to tip. She was going to fall and there was nothing she could do about it. Her hand let go of the shelf and her arms wheeled as she threw herself back, hoping the chair would right itself, but it didn't, and she was falling through the air, about to hit the floor with a bone-crunching thud.

But she didn't.

They felt like arms, the things that caught her at the shoulders and behind her knees. Warm, solid arms that set her gently on her feet. Her heart pounded; the empty room spun around her.

Amelia screamed.

CHAPTER THREE

The Thief

AMELIA INHALED, TAKING A FULL, deep breath of the familiar. She hadn't recognized much of the town, having only driven through it once, and what little she remembered wasn't much to look at anyway, but the bookshop was the same kind there'd been back home. The signs telling people where to find fiction and cookbooks and travel guides were exactly the same. There was a corner stocked with toys next to the picture books, just like the one she'd played in while Mum and Dad browsed when she was younger.

Owen ran past her, presumably to find the newest book in the series he'd been reading; he'd talked about nothing else in the car. Of course he'd decided to interfere with Amelia's outing, which was supposed to be her and Dad, asking if he could come before Amelia had even put her shoes on. And Dad had said yes! Amelia had almost decided she didn't want to go to the bookshop after all, but she'd needed to. And now she was glad she'd come. It was just like home.

Mr. Howling put his hand on Amelia's shoulder. "The dictionaries and thesauruses are over there," he said, pointing. "Do you want help picking one out?"

"No, thanks, I can find what I need," said Amelia. She wanted to look around for a bit first anyway.

And she wasn't getting a thesaurus anymore.

"Okay," said her father. "Find me when you're ready."

She waited until he was eagerly browsing a shelf of the mystery novels he loved so much. Owen was busy reading the first few pages of something.

The people who worked here looked like the ones at the bookshop back home. They weren't the same people, obviously, but they wore identical shirts, and so she knew what to look for. "Excuse me," she said, hoping they'd be as helpful as the ones back home too.

A man stopped putting new books on a shelf and turned around. He had a very long beard, and his arms were covered with tattoos revealed by rolled-up sleeves.

He looked a bit like a pirate from a story Amelia had read once, but the pirate had been a friendly one, and the man smiled at her. "Can I help you?" he asked. "Children's books are over there."

"I know," said Amelia. "I need a book about ghosts."

The man crossed his arms, a thinking sort of expression crossing the bits of face that weren't hairy. "Like, ghost stories?"

"Only if they're true. I need to know how to catch one." Catch, like it had caught her when she'd fallen from the chair.

"Do you think your house has a ghost?" he asked, smiling.

"I think my house *is* a ghost," she said. It was the only way to explain it. Yes, she'd seen something, a shadow of a man, but the whole house had feelings.

His eyebrows rose. "Oh. Well, follow me. We do have a small supernatural section over here. . . ." He led her to a low, double-sided bookcase and bent down, searching. "I see people buying this sometimes," he said. Its glossy cover caught the light. *Haunted?* the title asked. Amelia liked the question mark. She had a lot of question marks herself. Such as why the ghost had saved her from the fall, and why, after making two appearances that day, first in the attic and later in the

42

library, the ghost hadn't shown itself at all since. Below the jaunty title it read: *How to Discover Malevolent Spirits and Set Them Free.*

She took the book from the bookseller and flipped through the pages. Yes, this seemed perfect. "I'll take it," she said. The man nodded. Her father had given her the promised double pocket money before they'd left the house, and she fished for it as she followed him to the till. A moment later a glossy bag hung from her hand.

Dad was still looking at the mysteries, but Amelia wanted to get back to the house now. She had an actual mystery to solve. "I'm ready," she said. He saw the bag and humphed in surprise.

"Which one did you get?"

Amelia didn't really want to show him. Mum might've told Dad about Amelia saying the house was haunted, since her parents were so keen on talking about her when she wasn't around. But not showing him would make him suspicious. Reluctantly, she gave him the bag and held her breath as he withdrew the book from it.

"This isn't a thesaurus," he said. Her dad was very clever, and spent all day at work doing very clever things with computers, but sometimes he could be very silly.

"I know that," she said. "This is the book I want."

"Are you sure? It looks like it might give you nightmares. It would give *me* nightmares."

"It won't," Amelia insisted. She hadn't had any nightmares since the ghost revealed itself.

She hadn't had any dreams at all since she moved into the house.

"If you're sure," said her father. "Owen, time to go."

She read her book all the way home, even though it made her feel a bit carsick, squinting at the small letters as the they moved through the traffic. She read it while climbing the porch stairs, and as she stepped into the library, and as she settled herself in her favorite chair. The one she'd fallen from was still near the shelves; Mum hadn't noticed she'd moved it. Mum hadn't heard her scream that day either; all that paper had swallowed the noise, and Mum had been somewhere else in the enormous house.

She'd only been scared for a minute. Now she was determined to get to the bottom of this.

The library door opened. Amelia quickly looked up, not entirely sure who—or what—she expected to see, but it was only Owen, carrying the book he'd run off to read at the shop. He flopped down in one of the other chairs. Amelia marked her place in her own book with her finger.

"Did you buy that?" she asked. "I didn't see you buy that."

"None of your business," he said, glaring at her.

Amelia gasped. She knew he hadn't bought it, and stealing a book was about the most wrong thing she could think of. "I'm telling Mum."

"Go ahead."

Mum and Dad were sitting at the kitchen table, drinking coffee, when Amelia stormed in. "Owen has a book he didn't pay for," she said. Both looked up at her in surprise, and a frown of disappointment creased her mother's lips. Good, let them be disappointed in him. "He *stole*—"

"I bought it for him, Amie," interrupted her father. Amelia's angry insides popped like a balloon, only to reinflate again. Wait one second. How was *that* fair? She had to earn extra pocket money by heaving boxes up three flights of stairs, and he got a book for doing nothing? But she knew if she said so, her parents would remind her how much Owen and Matthew and Lavender had been through, blah blah, and she knew that was true, but still, couldn't anything just be fair for once?

"Fine," she said through gritted teeth. "I'm going outside."

"Stay on the property, please," said her mother, a little sadly. Amelia left the kitchen as quickly as she'd come, though she did not immediately go outdoors. She turned in the entrance hall and ran up the stairs two at a time to her room to fetch the notebook she kept on her bedside table.

It wasn't there. With a fresh wave of annoyance at Owen or Matthew, one of whom was still messing with her things . . .

She looked at the cover of the book in her arms. Perhaps it wasn't one of them after all. Not that she would apologize to Owen for accusing him of that, either.

"All right, ghost, where did you put my notebook? I need it."

It didn't answer. She hadn't expected it to. Apparently it was helpful enough to stop her from breaking bones, but not helpful enough to tell her where her notebook was.

Eventually she found it neatly tucked away on a shelf, and with it and *Haunted?* she ventured outside.

It was a lovely day; she hadn't really noticed on the way to the bookshop, but all the days here so far had been. Long hours of sunshine, with the merest hint of crispness whispering of chilled nights and frosted mornings to come. Soon it would be Amelia's favorite time of year, and that made this *almost* even better. A held breath that would soon release, blowing cool wind across the treetops. Soon it would be her favorite time of year, and she'd be forced to spend it here. All right, it would probably be quite something when the leaves began to turn; there were far more trees here than back home. She could fit twenty of her perfect old house and its garden inside the rotten brick walls that ran around the veritable—that was a good word—forest that surrounded her new, horrible, haunted house.

She stood in the shade of the trees right on the line where the verdant—she'd read the *V* section of her dictionary recently—lawn ended and the woods began, and looked up at the house. Fine, it wasn't horrible, it was really rather curious and unusual-looking, but it was pretending to be something it wasn't.

It was pretending to be a normal house, all innocent windows and blameless bricks.

Amelia squinted at it. "I'll discover your secrets, you know," she said.

Again, no answer came.

The trick was to be clever. She knew all about investigations; she and Izzy had solved all kinds of mysteries.

Mysteries they'd made up, true, but that wasn't the point. The point was that she simply needed to look at the problem sensibly. Her new book advised making a list of all unusual occurrences, looking for patterns in the haunting. Amelia sat against a tree, facing the house so she could see it quite clearly, and opened her notebook.

House appears to be haunted.

Some of the rooms are freezing and some are hotter than that holiday we took in Greece.

No matter where you are, it doesn't feel empty.

Serious investigations called for. Recommended: Inspect every room and make detailed notes. For accuracy, start in the basement and work upward.

She was going to need a warm jumper. And possibly a snack. She and Izzy had discovered years ago that the most important part of any adventure was to do it on a full stomach. There was nothing more rubbish than having to stop for food right when things were getting exciting. Breakfast lingered in her belly from before the trip to town, but it wasn't a small house. Looking at it now, it loomed over her in precisely the same fashion it had when she'd first arrived. Knowing she didn't want to be here. Knowing she didn't like it.

And it knew her better than it had that first day, so

it seemed to say more now, with its door-mouths and window-eyes half hidden by winking shutters.

Come and find me, smirked the hateful house. *You're a clever girl. Come and discover what I'm hiding.*

Just as she had when she'd first stepped reluctantly from the car, stretching her aching legs after the cramped miles, she stuck her tongue out. She would, thank you very much. Oh yes, she would. It was only a pile of bricks and wood. She was a pile of brains with nothing better to do.

"Back so soon?" Mrs. Howling asked. Amelia had made all the notes she could think of outside.

"I wanted a jumper," she said. "And an apple."

Surprise crossed Mrs. Howling's face. "I didn't think it was chilly. I suppose it's that changeable time of year. Get whatever you like, sweetheart. There are apples in the pantry and"—her voice dropped to a whisper—"some of those biscuits you like tucked behind the cereal."

Finally, something was unfair in Amelia's favor. "Thanks, Mum."

The door to the basement was firmly closed to keep the cold down there, or it'd freeze the whole house. Amelia reached for the knob . . . and stopped. She closed her eyes and felt the house around her. It gusted its breath across the back of her neck, blow-ing the hairs there straight on end. She waited until Mum was clattering pots and pans, which clatter no matter how carefully they're arranged in a cupboard, and turned the handle.

Wintry air swirled around her. Amelia quickly flicked the light switch before closing the door. She wasn't afraid of the dark, but she didn't want to be smothered by it down here where it was damp and cold as well.

The stairs creaked. She knew that. She'd been down here before.

What was odd . . .

What was odd was . . .

Amelia turned sharply on a step in the middle of the staircase. Her bottom half was colder than her top half, but that wasn't what sent a spider-legged shiver up her spine.

The steps creaked, yes. But steps don't usually creak a second *after* they've been trodden on. Perhaps the cold made the wood act different. Perhaps.

She placed a foot on the stair below. It creaked, but softly, as if it had an opinion but wasn't sure it should share it.

Two steps above, that stair creaked too.

The air in the basement smelled of the hour before

snow. Amelia remembered the first time last year she had . . . There wasn't a word for glimpsing something with your nose, was there? If there was such a word, that's what she'd mean: glimpsing a whiff of this exact scent a few moments before bed, awaking to a blanket of snow. She and Izzy had immediately turned it all into snowmen and snowwomen and forts for them to live in. None of their masterpieces had been very large—it hadn't snowed *that* much—but they were masterpieces nonetheless. When their fingers were numb and their noses red, Izzy's mum had made them hot chocolate with marshmallows.

The basement smelled just like that. Amelia ran down to the bottom as fast as she could, the creaks coming at almost the right times. Fumbling the pencil in her cold hand, she scribbled her observations in her notebook. She poked around a bit to see if there was anything else worth writing down, but everything she saw or felt could be filed under *cold* or *creepy*, and she'd covered those pretty well already.

It was important to be thorough. It was also import-ant not to freeze to death.

Back upstairs the ground floor felt like the first spring morning after endless long, dark months. Pleasantly warm, but not hot. Mum was still in the kitchen, baking fresh bread. Mouth watering, Amelia took the long way round to the conservatory, through the entrance hall and the empty sitting room.

There might not be a word for glimpsing something with your nose, but there was a word for this: *petrichor*. The scent of the earth after rain. Mum must have watered the plants this morning.

Besides the library, this was the room Amelia liked most. Not that she liked anything about the house, but she hated the conservatory and library the least. They were the friendliest rooms. And though she felt just as watched here as in any of the others, it worried her less, for some reason.

She sat on one of the wicker chairs. The green glass windows filtered the sun, made her feel as if she were just under the surface of the clearest, bluest ocean. Plants and miniature trees cast spiky shadows on the flagstones. That peace lily was a bird in flight, that cactus a woolly-haired man, waving his arms.

That night Amelia slept with the light on. Her notebook sat on her nightstand, filled with observations about the house. She'd gone all the way up to the attic.

And was sure the ghost had followed her the entire time.

"Poor thing," said her father, drawing his hand back from the switch on the lamp. "I knew that book would give you nightmares. Do you want me to take it downstairs?" It was on her nightstand too.

"No, it's all right," said Amelia.

"Are you sure?"

"I'm sure."

She wasn't afraid of the dark.

Shadows were a different story, and while there were still odd shapes around her room and on the walls, she could at least see what they were. There are different kinds of darkness, and they can hide inside one another, turn an innocent bedroom into a puzzle box of fright.

The moon had begun to fall by the time her eyelids fell with it, and in the morning she was as tired as if she hadn't slept at all. Matthew and Owen were being very loud in the sitting room, but the kitchen was quieter. Lavender babbled softly to herself on the floor.

"No more ghost stories for you," said Mum, setting a plate of toast down in front of Amelia. "Your father told me you needed to sleep with the light on. You look exhausted, Amie."

"Has he left for work already?"

"Yes. He told me to tell you he loves you."

"There's something in this house," Amelia said. "It's not just because I don't like it here. Haven't you noticed that the basement is freezing as winter, but our bedrooms feel like the desert?"

"It's an old house, Amelia. The heating was probably put in before *I* was born, let alone you. You're right, though, that we still need to get someone in to look at it."

"You don't feel like the house is always watching you?"

"I haven't had a moment alone in weeks; someone's always watching me. But I don't think it's the house," said Mrs. Howling firmly, "and neither should you."

If Amelia said she kept seeing shadows shaped like people, Mum would have an explanation for that, too.

"If it would make you feel better to read about the house, Hugo did say it's mentioned in a book somewhere. He told me on the phone when they were buying it. I don't know if you remember, but your uncle was an architect. That's someone who designs buildings for a living."

"I know what an architect is, Mum. I'm all the way up to the *W*s." Amelia yawned.

Mrs. Howling smiled. "Right. Well, apparently the house has some unusual features, but he didn't tell me what they were, just that they were why he and Marie wanted the place. The two of them were very excited about it. It's sad they didn't get to live here very long." Amelia's mother stopped and pressed her fingers to her eyes.

"What book?" demanded Amelia, jumping up from the table, ready to run to the library and search for it.

"I'm not sure. I don't even know if it's here, Amie, but I'll try to find it for you, I promise. It might be in the room upstairs he used as an office. For now, finish your breakfast. We need to go out."

"Where?"

"I need to take Owen and Matthew to speak to someone. When you suffer a loss like they have, it can help to speak to a person, like a friend, who knows about these things."

"I can stay here," offered Amelia. "I just want to read. I'll even watch Lavender," she added, hoping this would convince her mother.

"I don't think so. Eat up."

Amelia was finishing the last bite of her toast when Mrs. Howling bustled back into the kitchen, looking for her keys and shooting Amelia an exasperated look that Amelia did not deserve. She hadn't hidden them. But she wanted Mum to look for the book later, when she had time, and so Amelia helped with the search, eventually excavating them from under a pile of Lavender's toys.

The front door stuck when they tried to leave. Mrs. Howling checked twice that it was unlocked, huffing and wrenching the doorknob with one hand while she clutched Lavender to her hip with the other. A gust of wind blew in when the wood finally relented, whipping up the trees as far as Amelia could see down the long driveway.

Owen ran past her to take the front seat. Matthew followed him because Matthew often did. Amelia was the last to step outside, the last to leave the house. The door slammed so suddenly behind her that she only narrowly got her fingers out of the way. She stood on the step and considered running back inside for her notebook. It was worth writing this down.

The house was *angry*.

She thought back. There had always been someone here, at least since she'd arrived. This was the first time the house would be completely empty.

"Amie, stop dawdling; we're going to be late!" called Mum from the car.

"We're coming back," Amelia whispered to the bricks.

The house shuddered in the wind and . . . relaxed. That was the only word for the feeling, and a feeling for which Amelia had no word filled her. It was almost pride, but not exactly. She was the only one who knew there was something odd about the house; she was the only one who would have thought to soothe it.

Amelia glared at the back of Owen's head, hating him anew. The front seat had always been her spot when it was just her and Mum in the car. Pressed against the window, far as she could get from Matthew in the middle and Lavender in her special car seat, Amelia felt the house growing smaller and smaller behind her.

Her eyes fell shut.

Dreams chased one another through the landscape of sleep, bright and detailed as oil paintings. A touch jolted her awake as she moved from one to the next, Mum's hand on her shoulder. The glass building to which they had come was dull in comparison to the lingering pictures in Amelia's mind, even as it gleamed in the sunshine. She paid no notice to it, or to the long white corridor, or to her mother offering to take her and Lavender for ice cream after the boys had been shown inside a small room filled with toys.

When she woke again, they were back at the house. She was almost too awake now, and a suspicion itched at her as she fidgeted behind her mother. It was taking too long for Mrs. Howling to open the door, and Amelia needed to get inside, needed to get to her new book. She ran inside the second she could, up the stairs two at a time, past the horrid letters on her bedroom door. The book was where she'd left it.

Her eyeballs scanned the pages so quickly they began to ache. Please, let it say something.

It did.

> *. . . One of the most reported observations is that of sleep disturbance. Residents of dwellings where Presences are suspected frequently note sleeping far less or more than usual, as well as being awoken from deep sleeps by unexplainable noises, and varying types of dream interference . . .*

Amelia slammed the book shut with such a snap it echoed around the room. If it had been anything but a book, she would've thrown the object in her hands against the wall.

The house thought *it* had been angry when everyone left it. The house had nothing on Amelia.

CHAPTER FOUR

The Door to Nowhere

THE HOUSE—OR SOMETHING LURKING inside it—was stealing her dreams.

She couldn't say so; it would sound ridiculous to everyone else. Mum already had an explanation for all the strange things, even if those explanations were assuredly wrong.

Investigations were called for. Furious as she was, Amelia flopped back onto her pillow and resolutely closed her eyes.

But sleep wouldn't come, as sleep often doesn't when it's a wanted thing. A sly fox that can't be trapped, but must venture of its own accord near enough to be caught.

Well, it couldn't hide forever, and that night Amelia would know for certain what she already knew for certain, deep inside.

The house was stealing her dreams.

Houses could not speak, or feel, or wish, or steal; they were piles of bricks and wood and glass. This was all ridiculous. And yet the house was glad to have them home, that Amelia had kept her promise made on the doorstep.

She was sorry she'd said it, now.

Matthew and Owen were talking in low voices behind Owen's closed bedroom door. Amelia raised her hand to knock, then thought better of it. They might laugh at her if she asked. Or they might say they were dreaming just fine, thank you, and she'd have to wonder why it was only her.

"Give me my dreams back, stupid house," she muttered under her breath, and turned for the stairs. If she couldn't find out more about the dreams, she could learn more about the house.

"Shhh," said Mrs. Howling from the sitting room as Amelia reached the bottom. Lavender was asleep on the couch, the green air from the conservatory wafting gently across her face.

Of course, *she* hadn't needed to be woken when they

got out of the car. Mrs. Howling had carried her inside, special little Lavender, who got to be held whenever she wanted. Amelia watched her, scowling. She couldn't remember at what age her own dreams had begun, but she knew the exact date they'd stopped. The same day she'd arrived here. Was Lavender dreaming now? Was it truly just Amelia's that had gone missing, like old socks and favorite marbles?

"Mum, will you find that book for me, please?"

"I will in a bit, Amie, all right?" her mother answered, leaning back against the cushions. "I'd love five minutes of quiet. It's probably in his office. Where are the boys?"

"They went upstairs."

"Good. They might need some time to themselves too. Please, go amuse yourself for now."

She said it as if Amelia had done anything *but* amuse herself since she came here. Not once had she played with her cousins or asked Mum to climb one of the many trees with her, and Dad didn't get back until almost dinnertime every evening.

Fine, she would amuse herself. Back upstairs she went, creeping past Owen's bedroom to a door she'd not yet opened. She'd been told not to. The house gathered itself around her, waiting. A living, feeling house, breathing with its conservatory-lungs, thinking with its library-brain. Although if the library was its brain, it was in the wrong place. The library should be in the attic, which was empty of all but boxes and sunlight. And strange chalk markings on the floor.

Inside Uncle Hugo's office was the kind of stillness where seconds last as long as minutes, minutes as long as hours. The kind of stillness that hadn't been disturbed in a long time. Probably not since the night the silence began. Pens were still scattered haphazardly across a large wooden desk, though also on the desk was a fairly ugly mug that was clearly supposed to hold them. There was another, funny-looking desk, its top at an angle and its legs tall enough that Amelia had to stand on tiptoe to see the paper spread on it.

As she'd reminded Mum, she knew what an architect did. It was no surprise, then, that the drawing on the paper looked to be of a house. Hard lines defined each room, with little notches in most of them for doorways. Her finger hovered over what was clearly a staircase, careful not to smudge the pencil.

The curtains were mostly closed; the room was dim and full of shadows. Amelia squinted, looking for faces, and thought, replaying her days in her mind.

It wasn't odd that her uncle had a drawing of a house

on his funny desk; that had been his job. It *was* odd that he had a drawing of *this* house. This house was already finished. Had he meant to built another exactly like it? There was enough room on the land outside, if some of the trees were cleared away, but why?

The drawing was only of the ground floor: the conservatory that smelled of petrichor, the kitchen where she ate with Mum and Dad and the others, the library where someone had caught her from a fall. There were the stairs to the basement, which creaked out of time.

Amelia lifted the corner of the paper. Yes, there was another beneath, showing the bedrooms and bathrooms and the room she stood in at that very moment. The fire of anger had dimmed slightly in her belly, distracted by her mission, but it reignited at the sight of her room, a rectangle right under her finger. She was supposed to have dreams in that room, and the house was stealing them.

She needed to find that book. Books always held the answers. Her new one, from the bookshop, was helpful, but it didn't know everything. Sometimes she needed more than one, like when she read a word she didn't know and had to use her dictionary to help her understand the story.

Before she moved her hands from the papers on her

uncle's desk, something else on the drawing caught her eye. The door through which she had come was closed behind her, a clear line on the page, a notch like all the others.

And there was another. She looked up at the wall. Sure enough, there it was. Right between the windows, half hidden by the nearly closed curtains, was a door, which made no sense. This room was upstairs, and there was no balcony on the other side. Maybe once there had been, and something had happened to it?

Slowly, as if the door would blow open and suck her out to fly through the air, Amelia approached, reaching out for the handle. It turned easily. Well-oiled hinges opened without a single creak. Disappointed, she frowned at the plain bricks on the other side. Just an ordinary door, then, that had perhaps once led to something but since been walled off.

"What are you doing in here?" yelled Owen. Amelia jumped, spun in the air to face him. He stood in the doorway to the hall, glaring. She glared right back.

"I was looking for something," she said, as if she had to explain herself to him.

Owen's knuckles gleamed white on the doorknob. "I told you that you weren't allowed in here," he said, his voice shaking. "This is my dad's. All his things are here."

"I'm not hurting them," said Amelia, who didn't want to lie and say she hadn't been touching them at all. "And I live here too. I can go anywhere I want."

That's right, said the house's voice in her head. *This is your home now. You belong here.*

"Shut up!" said Amelia.

"You shut up!" shouted Owen.

"Oh!" Amelia blinked. "No! I didn't mean you. It was . . ." She didn't want the voice. She didn't want this to be her home. She didn't want the house stealing her dreams. And she didn't want Owen telling Mum she was being mean to him when she wasn't, not this time. She hated the house more than she hated him, and she needed to know everything about it in order to hate it properly. "I'm sorry," she said. "I was looking for a book."

Owen was not in a forgiving mood. "Oh, because you don't have enough of those," he answered, sneering. "Finished reading your dictionary, have you?"

Now she did want to tell him to shut up. She bit her tongue. "My mum said this house was in a book somewhere, and she thought it was in here. You could've told me when I asked if there was anything weird about the house, you know. You could've told me about the book, or that funny door that doesn't go anywhere."

Owen shrugged, still scowling. "So it's a strange old house. I don't know why you care so much; it isn't your house. If I show you the book, will you leave my dad's things alone?"

"Yes."

He released the doorknob and stomped into the room, plucking a book from the top of a teetering pile on a stool near the big, flat desk. "He showed me once. I didn't read it. I didn't want to move here either, but Mum and Dad made us."

"Thank you," said Amelia stiffly. It wasn't easy to make her mouth form the words. "You really didn't want to move here?"

"It's a stupid house with a stupid name and I had to leave all my friends. So I know how you feel."

He sounded more sad than angry, and Amelia's chest twinged. "I don't know how you feel," she said.

"It's horrible. I wouldn't even wish it on Trevor at school, and I hate him. I feel . . . I feel like I'm forgetting them already. You should hope you never know what it's like. Now get out."

"All right." She was torn between asking him more questions and finding more answers, but he made the decision for her. As soon as she was out of the office, he closed the door and ran back to his own room.

Amelia took the book to her window seat, staring at the cover. *Unusual Homes of the British Isles,* it said, with the author's name underneath. She opened it and began to search.

> *Nudiustertian House, in the south, is another one of these architectural oddities. Built sometime in the mid-nineteenth century, it follows the same pattern as the other so-called calendar houses that have been discovered either by accident or because clues to their nature were left in obvious places. Like all the others, its design is entirely unique, though once you are aware of the details you're looking for, the similarities become obvious. Not as much research has been done on Nudiustertian House as some of the others, due to it having been almost continuously occupied since it was built, but there is certainly no doubt that it is a calendar house. Signs show that at some stage, residents have modified the design, removing the formal dining room and adding a conservatory. However, accidentally—or perhaps not—the important number of rooms was preserved*

after this change. The twelve main spaces are there to represent the months of the year; the four floors, including attic and cellar, clearly encapsulate the seasons. Other numbers that have significance in the passage of time are quite obviously in existence; indeed, if this particular house could be fully scrutinized, it may well be found to be the most complete calendar house still standing, perhaps the most complete ever constructed. It is said too that the property contains exactly three hundred sixty-five trees, but to date no one has managed to count them all with any degree of certainty.

What remains from study of these unusual homes is that scholars still do not know why they were built, what architectural craze it was that led to this becoming a fashion. . . .

Amelia raised her eyes, scanning the trees outside. How many leaves were on three hundred sixty-five trees?

A calendar house. She reached for her dictionary, hefted it onto her lap.

Nudiustertian meant "of or relating to the day before yesterday." "A stupid house with a stupid name," Owen had said, but the name meant something. It was as tied to time as the house itself, and the explanation of the house in the book was the first thing that had made any sense since she arrived. A floor for every season: That was why the basement was freezing cold, her bedroom burning hot. It was why the conservatory leaked the scent of spring into the kitchen and sitting room and library, and why the attic smelled of burning leaves. Mum was wrong; it had nothing to do with it being an old house with old, clunky heating, and they didn't need a repairman to look at it.

She'd tried investigating before, but she hadn't known enough. Now she did. Amelia found her notebook and flipped to the page where she'd written down her questions. With the help of *Unusual Homes of the British Isles,* she wrote down every number she could think of that had something to do with a calendar. There were seven days in a week, and four or five weeks in a month. Twenty-eight, thirty, or thirty-one days in a month too, twenty-nine every fourth February. Fifty-two weeks in a year, and twelve months. Four seasons, but she already knew where those were in the house. And the book said there were twelve rooms, but she'd count them for herself.

She wouldn't count the trees, at least not yet. That was going to take a long time, and she'd have to figure out a way to make sure she didn't count any of them twice, mark the trunks somehow. Chalk would work, so long as it didn't wash off in the rain before she was done.

The notebook tumbled from her lap. On her knees she crawled along the window seat, pushing books out of the way, searching.

There it was. Smudged by the movement of the curtains, small enough so as to go unnoticed. *41*.

Someone had counted the windows. Uncle Hugo, when he was making his drawings?

There was plenty to be getting on with indoors. Sixty seconds in a minute and minutes in an hour, twenty-four hours in a day. More numbers than she'd ever thought of, really, but then she'd never much cared to think of them. Words had always been friendlier to Amelia, full of meaning.

That was then. These numbers had meaning, each measuring out important details, and that made them the same as words, didn't it? The right words and the right numbers for the right things

Her uncle's drawings were still in his office; she could simply go and count things on them. They didn't show everything, though, and anyway, actually exploring the house was more fun. That made it more of an investigation.

Pencil behind her ear, Amelia left her room, deciding once more to begin at the very bottom of the house and work upward, and already wearing a warm jumper to protect her from the basement's wintry cold.

That was one part she didn't understand: the four floors for the four seasons made sense, but how had whoever constructed the house fixed it so each was the right temperature?

The faces, and the arms that had caught her, were the other parts she didn't understand. Nowhere in *Unusual Homes of the British Isles* did it mention calendar houses being haunted, and nowhere in *Haunted?* did it mention calendar houses at all.

But she had one piece of the puzzle. One thread, and if she pulled, the mystery would unravel. One day, someone would write another book about unusual houses, and she would be named as the person who had fully studied Nudiustertian House, discovered it to be the most complete calendar house there was.

It would be a good idea, sometime between now and then, to learn how to properly pronounce it.

Amelia stood with the frozen pipes and shivering shadows at her back and counted the stairs back up to the ground floor. The number she wrote down in her notebook didn't seem to mean anything, but there were more stairs in the house and a few outside leading up to the porch. Perhaps they added up to a certain number. She counted the library and the sitting room, peeked into the kitchen, where her mother was leaning over something at the counter while Lavender chewed on a brightly colored book at the table.

"Amelia!" called Mrs. Howling, and Amelia jumped, stumbled through the doorway. Mrs. Howling jumped too, her hand over her chest. "Oh! You were right there."

"Um, yes," said Amelia, relieved that her mother didn't actually have eyes in the back of her head. That was just a thing they said about parents.

"You have a letter," said Mrs. Howling, a smile on her face. The thing she'd been leaning over was a stack of envelopes, and she took the one from the top, holding it out to Amelia. "I think it's from Isabelle."

She'd answered! Both Amelia and Isabelle had been told they were allowed to use the computers to write each other, but as Amelia had told her father, getting proper letters was so much more exciting. Plus, no one else could read them this way, and letters should be private things.

Amelia took the letter, dodging Lavender's grabby, sticky hands as she sat at the table to read it.

72

Impatiently, she tore open the envelope, pulled out a sheaf of pages. The first part of the letter was all about going back to school, who her new teachers would be and who she was going to sit with at lunch now that Amelia was gone. A great sadness filled Amelia's chest at all the names she recognized and a few she didn't, new people Izzy had met at the swimming pool or the park over the summer. Tears began to prickle her eyes, and so the words on the next page were a blur. Amelia blinked several times to get them to come into focus.

She wished she hadn't. She wished she hadn't opened the letter at all.

> *. . . The pond is full of frogs, but I don't know how much longer I'll be allowed to visit them. The new family moving into your house has a little boy, and I overheard them telling Mum they'll have to put a fence round it so he doesn't fall in. Why does a boy have to move in next door? He's not even the right age to play with. Mum said your mum and dad were lucky to sell it so quickly in this market, whatever that means, and that I don't get to choose who lives there. I think that's rubbish.*

New family. Amelia dropped the letter, her hands as hot as if the paper had been on fire.

"Amie?" said Mrs. Howling, looking up at the sound of the letter hitting the floor, pages scattering in different directions. Lavender grabbed one of them and tore it cheerfully in half. "Amie, what is it?"

"You sold my house!" yelled Amelia. "How could you? How could you sell my house?"

Mrs. Howling's face fell. "Oh, Amie. I'm so . . . This isn't . . . Come back; let's talk about this properly."

"No!" Amelia was almost at the stairs. "I don't want to talk to you. I don't want to talk to anyone! Leave me alone!"

She ran, up, up, counting the stairs forgotten, running just to get as far away as she could from Mum, from that horrible letter, from her father's key in the lock, home from work. The scent of burning leaves hit her nostrils as she slammed the attic door behind her. Too much had happened today; it couldn't possibly have all fit into the hours since she awoke from a terrible night's sleep. She flung herself to the floor beneath the oddly shaped window, tears spilling onto her knees.

Something moved. A rustle, a crunch. A shadow in the corner was the shape of a man with wild hair.

"Are you all right?" it said, and the voice came inside her head, the same voice that had spoken to her since the day she first arrived. It cleared its throat. "Are you all right?" it repeated, the voice sounding normal this time, coming from the shadow itself. That wasn't normal at *all.*

Amelia opened her mouth to scream.

And changed her mind. She was tired of being surprised. Surprised by the house, surprised by her parents, and they hadn't been good surprises either. She wasn't going to give in this time.

CHAPTER FIVE

A Shadow Comes to Life

T HE SHADOW GREW, AND FROM it stepped a man, solid and real. The scream stayed on Amelia's lips, just in case she needed it. There should not be strange men in her house, and this one was really quite strange even without him being able to turn from a shadow into a man. He wore a dusty suit of some thick, old-fashioned material she couldn't name, and black shoes with pointed toes and silver buckles, and on one finger a heavy ring set with an amber stone. Beneath the wild hair, which hung down past his collar, his face was young and his eyes were very, very old.

"I knew it," whispered Amelia, folding her arms, swallowing the last of her tears. It was a lie, and she suspected he could perfectly well tell it was a lie. She had known there was something odd about the house, yes, and she had guessed it was haunted, and she'd found some of the clues, but she hadn't put them all together. If she'd tried, she wasn't sure she would have put them together in the shape of *him*.

"You thought I was a ghost," he said. "I am not a ghost. Don't be afraid. You've been looking for me, the only one in the house clever enough to see there was a mystery, and now that I'm here, you want to scream?"

It wasn't the first time Amelia felt the house could read her mind. It was the first time she was certain of it. She still wondered whether she ought to scream, but if she screamed, he would disappear. Mum might come running, and she would listen to what Amelia had to say and then think Amelia was making up stories about the house again because she was upset. Upset because Mum and Dad had *sold her house*. Amelia gritted her teeth.

"What are you, then, if you're not a ghost?"

The man—and, nonsensical as it seemed, he was a man, not the shadow he'd been moments before— paced the attic floor. He stepped over to the oddly shaped window. "There is no precise word for what we are," he said. "I have seen the books you have been reading, left out in the library or by your window.

Ghosts and bogeymen and all manner of things. I am not a ghost, and I am not a bogeyman, either, but if it is helpful for you to think of me as akin to those, you would not be far wrong."

"Wait," said Amelia. "'We'?"

"You are clever, aren't you? Good. Yes, I am not the only one, but we will get to that later. There is no sense in your learning their names before you learn mine." He turned from the window and stretched out an arm in its old, dusty sleeve. "Miss Amelia Howling, my name is Horatio. It is a pleasure to properly meet you."

Amelia shook his hand, out of politeness or reflex or fear, she wasn't entirely sure. His skin was cold, the silver ring colder. "You've been watching me, though," she said. "Are you a . . . bad man?" Her parents had told her not to speak to strangers, but Horatio didn't feel like a stranger.

He felt like the house.

Horatio looked horrified. "No, Amelia. I am not here to hurt you, I promise you that. I am here to tell you about my house."

"How can it be your house?" Amelia asked. "My aunt and uncle bought it. It's their house, or it was. I don't know who owns it now, but if they sold it to you before they died, why are we still living in it?"

Horatio began to pace again, fingers on his chin. Thinking. *Aha,* thought Amelia. *He has no answer to that.* It wasn't his house at all.

And, yet, it felt like his. Like him. It felt as if he'd been here since the beginning, or at least since Amelia arrived.

"When your parents buy you a birthday gift," he began, "who does it belong to?"

"Me," said Amelia, with absolutely no idea what that had to do with anything.

"But they bought it with their money."

Amelia did not like where this was going. "It's still mine," she insisted.

"All right. Then we are agreed that just because you have paid for something, that doesn't make it yours. It is not precisely the same as a birthday present, in fact it is somewhat the opposite, but the house is mine. Other people may buy and sell it to one another, but it is mine. I built it, and I don't ever leave it for long."

"So you have been living here while we have," said Amelia. "You are the shadow I keep seeing. You caught me when I fell."

"Indeed. Well done."

Amelia had lots of questions, but, as was almost always the case in her experience, one rose above the others. "Why?"

A wooden creak answered for him, a foot on the bottom step of the staircase up to the attic.

"Amelia?" her mother called.

Amelia looked from the doorway to Horatio. She watched as he turned from man to shadow, his finger at his lips. As if she hadn't shouted at her mother enough today, and perhaps she hadn't, for she was still simmering with anger, now Mum had gone and frightened Horatio away. But she didn't shout. Horatio's gesture of silence had been clear, and he would almost certainly know if she disobeyed it. If she told, he might not come back to answer her question, or any others she might think of. She was on the brink of having a secret far bigger and better than the one her parents had kept from her. A secret that would make her more special than Owen or Matthew or Lavender.

Horatio was gone. Amelia cast a last look into the corners of the attic, searching, not finding any of the telltale signs. She was certain he had not gone far, and the faster she got Mum to leave her be, the sooner he would come back.

She met her mother on the landing below, allowed herself to be steered into her bedroom, where her father was waiting. Lavender could be heard fussing from her bed across the hall, but for once Amelia's parents didn't run to her. Downstairs, Owen and Matthew were playing loudly. Amelia perched on her window seat. From the corner of her eye she saw the tiny *41* scrawled on the wall. She did not look at her parents.

"We're sorry, Amie," said her father.

"All right."

"It's too difficult and too expensive to keep two houses at once, sweetheart, especially when one is so far away," said her mother.

"All right."

"And we were waiting until we were absolutely certain before we told you." Mr. Howling ran a hand through his hair. That's what made it stick up all the time. "We simply didn't realize Isabelle would mention it in a letter."

Well, she had.

"It's time for another family to be as happy there as we were, Amie," said her mother. "And for us to be happy here."

"Fine." Amelia's eyes darted into the corners of the room, into the fireplace, searching for hints of Horatio.

"We know it's taking a lot of getting used to. Do you want to talk more about it?"

Amelia shook her head.

"Would you like to come downstairs to eat?"

Amelia shook her head again. She still didn't look at them, her eyes darting around the room and into the fireplace for hints of Horatio, but she let them hug and kiss her good night. It was actually much too early for Amelia's bedtime, but they seemed to guess that she didn't feel like returning downstairs, and this once they didn't press the issue. They collected Lavender and went to check on the boys, whose voices became mysteriously quieter.

So did Amelia's. "I'm alone," she whispered, though she was somehow quite sure that Horatio didn't need to be told about anything that happened inside the house. His house.

Did she believe that? That it belonged to him?

When she and Isabelle had done their experiments and solved their mysteries, the answer had not always been immediately obvious. Sometimes more information was necessary. The information she'd been trying to get by asking *why*, before her mother had called for her.

"Because," said Horatio, leaning on the mantelpiece as if he had always been there, and possibly he had, "I need people to live in my house."

Amelia jumped, but once again she refused to let

surprise overwhelm her. Especially not when she was so frustrated. It was a very frustrating thing to get a question answered and still not understand.

"One thing at a time," said Horatio. "I believe I must explain things in the correct order, as they were explained to me, long ago. You will come to know everything, Miss Amelia Howling; I promise that. First I will show you what the house is, and then I will show you what the house does, and then I will show you how the house does it."

Amelia waited.

And waited.

Horatio had said the best time to show her was when everyone else was out, so they might freely roam and talk through all the rooms. She already knew Mum would never agree to leave her home alone while she took the others somewhere, but Amelia had a plan.

Plans were excellent things. She had lots of practice from making them with Isabelle.

Finally the time came.

"What are you going to do today?" Mum asked over breakfast. "It's one of your last free days; back to school soon."

Amelia dropped her spoon into her third-favorite

kind of cereal. Owen and Matthew had polished off her first and second favorites. She'd completely forgotten about school, which was unlike her. Then again, before now she'd always been going back to her old school, like an old friend. This time she'd be somewhere new, and that really didn't bear thinking about.

Nevertheless, she would soon have much less free time. She had only a few days to let Horatio show her the mystery of the house, and as he'd said, she'd been the only one clever enough to work out that there was a mystery.

"I was thinking we could play outside," said Amelia, looking at Owen and Matthew. "All of us."

They were surprised, but not half as much as Mrs. Howling was. "I think that's a wonderful idea," she said. "Go have fun."

"You too, Mum," said Amelia.

"I need to get all your things ready for next week, Amie. Everyone's things. I've never done so much ironing."

"Please, Mum? Hide-and-seek is always better with more people."

Mrs. Howling put down the sponge she'd been using to wipe the counter. Lavender had made it sticky somehow. Lavender made everything sticky. She smiled. "Oh, all right, then. The ironing can wait, and Lavender could do with some fresh air."

Amelia smiled back.

Minutes later she was leading them into the woods. Which was foolish, probably, since Owen and Matthew almost definitely knew them better, but that only mattered if she was actually trying to hide. Amelia didn't stop in the first clearing she found, nor the second, but at the third she turned and grinned. "Here," she said, in a tone someone else might describe as bossy. She would describe that someone else as needing to mind their own business.

Mrs. Howling had put Lavender into a kind of rucksack, so that Lavender's eyes peeked over the top of Mrs. Howling's head. Giggling, she reached a tiny hand out to touch the bark of the nearest tree and drooled happily into Mrs. Howling's hair.

"Who starts?" asked Mrs. Howling. She hadn't yet noticed the drool. Owen had, Amelia saw, and was trying quite hard not to laugh. Amelia remembered the time they'd visited for Christmas, when Owen and Matthew were younger and Lavender not even born yet. Mr. Howling had gotten gravy on his nose, and she and Owen had giggled together at the table, waiting for her father to notice.

"Owen can," said Amelia. "He's the oldest. Except for you."

"Hey," said Mrs. Howling, but she ruffled Amelia's hair. "That all right with you, Owen?"

"Yes, Aunt Susan."

"All right. Some rules. Don't go off the property, and if you aren't found in five minutes, go back to the house. These trees are thick in places, and I don't want anyone getting properly lost. Agreed?"

"Agreed," said Matthew and Owen together.

"Yes, Mum," said Amelia, pleased. Her plan was going swimmingly so far.

"Count to thirty," she ordered Owen. "If you know how." He stuck his tongue out at her and covered his eyes.

The ground was soft with earth and leaves too green to crunch, all the better for sneaking away without Owen hearing which direction she'd gone in. She waited to see where Matthew headed, and her mother with Lavender, then ran off away from all of them. Now that she was deep inside the forest and having a proper look for the first time, she saw it had fewer trees than it seemed from the outside. When she sat at her window seat and watched them wave in the wind, it felt as if there must be thousands, but now she could see that it wasn't their number that made the forest appear so vast, but their size. They must have been growing forever. Maybe there were exactly three hundred sixty-five. She'd ask Horatio.

One of them had a split in the trunk that was, yes, just the right size for Amelia to fit inside.

She strained her ears and heard Owen shout that he was coming to find them. Holding her breath, staying as quiet as she possibly could, she waited.

And thought of Horatio, the shadow-man. She couldn't go back to the house quite yet, but soon, and she hoped he would be there when she did.

Owen's footsteps weren't as quiet as her own. Only another few seconds. If he found her too easily, he might complain to Mrs. Howling that she wasn't playing properly, even though the game had been Amelia's idea. Then again, if he took longer than the five minutes, everyone would have to go back to the house, and that would be terrible.

Amelia sneezed. *Whoops.*

"Found you!" Owen crowed. Amelia put on her best disappointed face and followed him back to where Mum, Matthew, and Lavender were waiting. Owen had found Matthew first, so it was his turn next, and again Amelia made it just exactly difficult enough for him to find her. Then it was her turn, and she found Mum and Lavender first, thanks to Lavender cackling excitedly at a bird.

"I'm very proud of you, Amie," said her mother, as she followed Amelia around looking for the boys. "This was a good idea; we're all having fun together."

"Thanks, Mum," said Amelia, pushing the leaves of a fallen branch out of the way and pulling a playfully scowling Matthew out. Owen was nearby, pressed flat against the bark of a tall, wide oak.

They'd all had a turn, now, except Mum, who wouldn't mind. It was time. "Mum? I'm actually not feeling well," said Amelia.

"Oh, dear, what's wrong?"

"I heard her sneezing," said Owen.

"And I heard her coughing," said Matthew.

Well. Maybe they could be helpful. Sometimes.

Mrs. Howling reached out and touched the back of her hand to Amelia's forehead. "You don't have a fever," she said. "All right, let's go back and get you into bed."

Owen and Matthew decided to be helpful again, though they didn't know it. Their faces fell, and Amelia shook her head. "I can go by myself," she said. "I'll just get in bed and read a book. Why don't you keep playing?"

Mrs. Howling frowned. "I don't know . . ."

"You're right out here, Mum. I'll be okay by myself, and I won't touch the stove or anything, promise."

"Are you sure, darling?"

"I'm sure," said Amelia.

"All right. We'll come back in an hour and check on you. It will be lunchtime then; I'll bring you some soup." Mrs. Howling covered her eyes, ignored Lavender clutching her hair with sticky fingers, and began to count to thirty.

Amelia walked until she was out of everyone's sight, and then she ran as fast as she could to the house, the trees thinning as she neared the garden. She had an hour. Would that be enough for Horatio to tell her the house's secret?

He was waiting for her in the kitchen, not a shadow but his suited, proper self. "Well done, Amelia," he said.

"Will you tell me now?"

"I will show you. Come, we do not have much time." Horatio strode from the kitchen and opened the door to the cellar. The stairs creaked and the bitter-cold air stung Amelia's lungs. The icicles on the pipes glinted in the light from the high, thin windows that were almost at the ceiling. "Winter," he said, spreading his hands.

"I know this part," said Amelia. "It's a calendar house. The ground floor is spring, which is why it smells of petrichor, and the bedrooms are summer and too hot to sleep in, and the attic is autumn that smells of burning leaves. How does it work? How did you do that?"

Horatio stared at her, impressed. "We will come to that," he said.

"Could you make my bedroom a little bit cooler so that it's easier for me to sleep?" Sleep. There was something about sleep. "And why don't I dream here?"

Horatio's eyebrow twitched. "Goodness," he said. "You are observant. Follow me." He took Amelia back up the stairs, into the entrance hall. "I assure you all the answers will come, when you know enough to understand them. I will see what I can do about a milder summer. You know the seasons; have you counted everything else? The twelve rooms, the seven fireplaces, the stairs and bannister railings and tiles around the doors?"

"Someone counted the windows," said Amelia, "but it wasn't me. There are markings underneath them; I'll show you." It was her turn to lead, to point out the *41* by her window seat, the *52* below the oddly shaped window in the attic. The number was more legible now; some things are easier to see when you know what they are.

"Your uncle," said Horatio, "before his untimely death. He believed he knew what the house was, but he viewed it, and the others of its kind, as an architectural curiosity, a thing built without purpose or reason."

"But there is a reason," said Amelia, looking away from the smudged blue chalk and into Horatio's ancient eyes.

"Oh, yes." Horatio smiled. "You know about calendar houses from your book. Well, welcome, Amelia, to mine. To anyone who knows what they do, and there are very few such people, I suppose there is only one way to describe them that you would understand."

Amelia did not at all like Horatio's patronizing tone. "I'm quite clever, you know," she said. "I can understand a great many things."

"I did not say you weren't, Amelia. I have seen your intelligence and curiosity for myself, and it is for that reason that you are the one I have chosen. You are a far better candidate than your cousins—the elder two, at least, and I do not wish to wait to see what kind of mind the baby has. I am merely saying that you are human, and thus I must use human terms, even if they are not precisely the right description, even if they do not fully capture the essence of the thing. The house, Amelia, is a time machine."

CHAPTER SIX

The Twenty-Fourth Door

S HE DIDN'T BELIEVE HIM. OF course she didn't believe him. Amelia sat on her window seat, eating the soup her mother had brought up, very studiously not believing him. Time machines weren't real, even if he'd been careful to explain that *time machine* wasn't precisely the right term. Using the wrong descriptions for things annoyed Amelia, but maybe she could allow it when the right ones didn't exist. Or maybe, since he'd obviously made up the story about the house, he should have put in the effort to make up a name for it as well.

The thing she didn't understand was *why*. It seemed an odd story to invent, and she said that as someone who had, alone and with Isabelle, invented a fair number of odd stories in her time. Mum and Dad hadn't believed most of them, just as Amelia didn't believe this one. It was fun, though, on those occasions when she could get Mr. and Mrs. Howling to think, for a moment, that there really *was* a dragon at the bottom of the garden. And a dragon at the bottom of the garden was as likely as this house being able to travel through time.

Or a man being able to turn into a shadow and back again.

There *was* something strange about him. Several somethings, if Amelia counted the feeling that he was the house, and that he knew everything that happened within it. Everything that happened in the forest outside too, unless he had been playing hide-and-seek with them. If he had, he'd been playing it very well.

Still, the house simply couldn't be a time machine. She wondered if she should tell Mum that there was a man living in their house, when Mrs. Howling came back upstairs to collect Amelia's soup bowl, but there were too many good reasons not to. For one thing it would look as if she cared about the house, or thought of it as hers in any way, and she didn't. The faraway house on the faraway hill was hers; it didn't matter that her parents had gone and sold it to someone else.

Anger bubbled anew in Amelia's belly, much hotter than the soup, not as hot as her bedroom. She hated it here. She hated her parents for not even asking her if it was all right to give her home away. She hated that she'd had to pretend to want to play with her cousins.

That was the other reason not to tell Mum about Horatio: He might be a silly secret, a lying secret, but he was *her* secret, and she would keep him. None of the others deserved to know about the shadow-man.

"You're not really sick, are you?" Owen barged in without knocking and threw himself on the end of Amelia's bed, nearly upsetting the empty soup bowl. It had been his running into the house that had scared Horatio away before Amelia could ask more questions. She narrowed her eyes at him.

"Of course I am," she said.

"No, you're not. I know what a fake sneeze sounds like."

"Oh yeah? Well, then why didn't you tell on me?"

"Because I'm not a tattletale like you," he retorted, folding his arms. "What were you doing here, all by yourself? Were you messing with my dad's things again?"

"No," said Amelia. That was true; she and Horatio hadn't gone into Uncle Hugo's office.

"Probably just wanted to read your dictionary in peace, then, I expect," he said, teasing.

A smile twitched on Amelia's reluctant lips. They used to have fun playing together. It wasn't the same as her and Izzy—she hadn't known him nearly as well—but he'd always been up for an adventure.

That had been when she'd known he was leaving, or she was going home again, and she'd have her house and her parents to herself. The house that wasn't hers anymore, and the parents who weren't only hers anymore.

"Go away," she told him, and pretended to be asleep when Mrs. Howling came in to take the tray away. A moment later a hand shook her shoulder.

"I know you're awake," said Horatio. Amelia startled.

"How?" she demanded. She thought she'd been doing a very good job.

"You are not dreaming," he said.

Amelia sat up. She was in just the mood to yell at something. "That's because I don't dream in this house," she said. "The house steals them. *You* steal them." She folded her arms across her chest and glared at him. Maddeningly, Horatio smiled.

"It was necessary," he said. "And I will show you why, but perhaps it is not so anymore. You will dream again tonight, if you wish, but your dreams are not our biggest problem. You do not believe me, Miss Amelia, and so I must prove to you that the house is what I say it is. Unless, of course, you don't wish to see. I may fade back into the shadows if I like, and you will never see me again. And if you try to tell anyone about me, no one will believe *you*."

There was a crackle of challenge in his old, dry voice. A breeze of fear and excitement raised the hairs on the back of Amelia's neck. "H-how will you show me?"

"The only way there is," he said. "I will prove it. Your mother thinks you to be asleep. We have some time—not enough for a truly grand adventure, but enough for this, I should say." Horatio appeared to think for an instant, then smiled wider and nodded to himself. He snapped his fingers. A fire bloomed to life in the fireplace, though there had been no logs in the grate. Amelia jumped, both from the surprise itself and from the extra blast of heat in the too-warm room. "Come with me," said Horatio, as if what he had done was in no way out of the ordinary. Perhaps, for him, it wasn't.

He led her next door, to the room that had been her uncle's office. Somehow, the moment they stepped inside, Amelia knew they weren't here for any of the books on buildings or the smudged blue drawings on the angled table. "The door," she said. The one that went nowhere.

"Oh, you are clever," said Horatio, who looked extremely pleased. "Do you know how many doors are in the house?"

"Twenty-four," said Amelia. "I counted them. This is the last one."

"Very good. I'm still not entirely sure why I put it in this room; it seemed like a wise idea at the time. I was young, still learning. No matter. Are you ready?"

"Yes," said Amelia. It may or may not have been a lie, but it couldn't be a *bad* lie, not when she didn't know the real answer. Her stomach fluttered.

"Close your eyes."

She heard the doorknob turn, felt a rush of fresh air. A dry, withered hand took hers, guiding her forward, and it was only then that Amelia remembered that the room was on the second floor of the house. Was she about to drop a long way to the ground?

No. But her feet were suddenly very cold and very wet. Amelia opened her eyes.

Winter. Winter everywhere, in the snow on the ground and the ice turning the trees to silver and the frost on the windows of her little house on its hill. If she ran around to the garden, she knew for sure the pond at the bottom would be frozen over. She had seen it happen every year of her life, watching the cold start at the muddy edges and creep slowly to the middle as Christmas came closer and closer.

Someone had hung a wreath on the front door. A different wreath from the one her mother had packed in a box and put on the truck that had carried Amelia's whole life away.

She didn't need to ask where they were. "*When* are we?" she asked instead.

"A much better question," said Horatio. One he didn't answer. "Would you like to go inside?"

"May we?"

"Of course. We will not be seen."

Amelia's socks squelched as they walked up the slippery, wet path. She cast her eyes back and forth, landed them on Isabelle's front door. Izzy! She could go and say hello! Or not, if Horatio said nobody would be able to see them.

A great sadness washed through her, carried into her skin by the bitter wind. The door was unlocked; Horatio turned the handle and Amelia followed him inside, keeping her eyes open this time, open enough to see that the carpet wasn't the green one she'd always known.

A small boy, maybe two or three years old, played on the floor of the living room. A woman sat at a computer, so they hadn't gone very far in time, even if they'd gone quite far in distance. A man sat in an armchair, reading a newspaper, the date printed clearly at the top. It was almost Christmas, but not just any Christmas. *Next* Christmas.

"So, you see," said Horatio. "Would you like to visit your former room? I believe humans are very attached to such things."

Amelia shook her head. Her face was wet with tears, wetter than her socks. These were the people to whom her parents had sold her house, a few months earlier according to the date on the paper. The people Izzy had told her about in the letter she sent in August. Amelia didn't want to look at them for another second.

She didn't want to look at anyone.

Amelia stayed in her room. Well, it wasn't her room, and she hated the stupid letters on the door, as if marking it with her name made it hers somehow whether she wanted it or not, but it was better than venturing out into the rest of the house. She still didn't want to see anyone, and at least she had a good excuse. A most curious thing had happened. When they arrived back at the house her feet had been bone-dry, and yet the shivers ran all the way from her toes up, up to the top of her head. Within an hour she was sneezing, and of course Mrs. Howling didn't want Amelia breathing her germs on the boys right before school was due to start. It was tempting to go and find them just for that reason.

That wasn't fair, however, and she knew it. Every time she began to think like this, she had to remind herself that it wasn't their fault their parents had died, and it wasn't even their fault she had been forced to come live here. But hating her cousins for those reasons wasn't fair, so she had to come up with other ones. Owen was older and thought he'd learned everything she didn't know in that one week before she'd been born, and Matthew was just younger enough to be annoying, and Lavender was too young to be fun. Those were good reasons.

Her parents were a different story. It wasn't their fault her aunt and uncle had died either, but it was their fault she had to be here. It was their fault they had sold her house to that other family, who looked so happy in it. Happy enough to change the carpets and sit reading the paper as if nothing in the world were wrong, though from the ones she had read, newspapers seemed to show everything in the world that was wrong.

They didn't have any headlines about a homesick girl, so they didn't know every tragedy.

The only good thing, the *only* one, was this house itself. Horatio had been telling the truth, or he had performed an impossible kind of magic, one even less likely than traveling through time. Could that be it? Had he shown her something that didn't really exist? Clearly he could do some very bizarre things. The fireplace was dark and cold once more, but Amelia stared at it from her bed and remembered the flames bursting to life.

It felt as if he was telling the truth, strange as it was. And it was a truth he had shared only with her, not with her stupid cousins or her mean parents. Horatio was the only person she wanted to see. She wanted him to show her more of what the house could do, take her somewhere else in time that wasn't as painful as her old house.

Next time she would remember to put on shoes, and perhaps a jumper. At least she would ask him what the weather would be like wherever they were going.

She'd ask him the next time she saw him, which she hadn't for three days now. There hadn't been the faintest whispering of a shadow except ordinary ones, no matter how hard she peered into the corners of the room.

A knock came. "Amie?" said her mother, opening the door without waiting for an answer. "I'm taking the others into town to buy school supplies. Are you feeling well enough to come?"

Amelia shook her head. Mrs. Howling's shoulders fell. "All right. I'll pick up things I think you'll like. Your father's outside doing some gardening if you need him."

"I'll be fine," said Amelia through gritted teeth. It came out rough, hoarse, but her mother either didn't notice or put it down to Amelia's sore throat, smiling sympathetically and closing the door. Her father used to do the gardening at her old house, trimming the weeds around the pond and tending to the flowers at the edge of the grass. Now another family lived there, and their little boy would probably stomp all over the lawn. They might even get rid of the pond out of fear the boy would drown in it. And her father was busy making the garden here look nice, as if nothing had changed and this was their home, when it wasn't and couldn't ever really be. It was Horatio's home, if it was anyone's; he only let them live here.

What had he said? He *needed* them to live here.

That was something else she needed to ask him about when she next saw him. A flicker of hope tickled at her. The house would technically be empty, apart from Amelia herself, and Horatio might be more likely to come if there wasn't anyone else around to catch them. She listened impatiently, straining her ears through the door and down the stairs for the sounds of Mrs. Howling getting Owen, Matthew, and Lavender ready and bundling them into the car. The engine disappeared into the trees down the long drive, and Amelia glanced around excitedly, feeling better than she had in days.

Sunlight streamed through the window, glinting off the shiny covers of her books on the seat. She waited.

And waited.

He didn't come. Not that day, or the next, when the house was full again and the boys were being unbearably loud, playing some stupid game in the sitting room. Fed up with staying in bed, Amelia hid herself away in the library, looking up after every line she read for a hint of Horatio.

Now she was angry at him, too.

"Amie!" Matthew shouted, bursting into the library. Owen was right behind him. "Want to come and play hide-and-seek again?" He plucked the book out of her hands, and a growling, snarling rage exploded from Amelia with a roar. She had tried to be nice to them, when she had to be, but how dare they? How dare *everyone*?

"No! Go away! I hate you and I don't want to play with you! And don't *ever* call me Amie!"

Footsteps came in a rush from the kitchen. "What is going on in here?" Mr. Howling demanded.

"Don't yell at my brother!" shouted Owen. Matthew had begun to cry. "I hate you too!"

"Everyone, quiet," ordered Mr. Howling. "Matthew, Owen, please go back into the sitting room. No, you're not in trouble—"

"Hey!" said Amelia.

"I said, quiet! Boys, go play, please. Susan?" he called louder. "Come here?"

Mrs. Howling passed the boys in the doorway as they left, Lavender on her hip. She looked from Amelia to Mr. Howling and quietly set Lavender down on the rug.

"What happened, Amelia?" asked her father.

Amelia scowled. "Matthew took my book away."

"That one?" he asked, pointing.

"Yes!" said Amelia, angry at so many things, but this time that he didn't seem to believe her. "He pulled it out of my hands."

"All right." Mr. Howling nodded. "I understand that made you angry, but that isn't a reason to say you hate someone, Amie. Matthew and Owen are your family. I know it's difficult, but you must learn to get along with them."

"We thought you were doing better," said Mrs. Howling, coming to sit next to Amelia, perching on the arm of the chair. "We all played together before you got ill."

Amelia's frown deepened. That had been before a lot of things; she'd had a very busy day that day. Before she got ill, yes, but also before Horatio had told her what the house was, and showed her what it could do, and taken her to see the new family living in *her* house. And before Horatio had disappeared, too. She'd only asked them to play as part of her plan.

Mr. Howling gave up waiting for an answer. "We may have pushed you too hard to adjust here," he said. "Your cousins have needed a lot of our attention, and you've always been such a grown-up girl that perhaps we've expected too much from you. School starts in a few days, and maybe things will be better then. So"—he glanced at Mrs. Howling, who nodded in a way that made Amelia *certain* they had been talking about her behind her back—"we will make you a deal, Amie. We will leave you alone to get used to things in your own way, and give you our time when you ask for it. You will still have to eat supper with everyone, but we won't force you into anything else. Apart from cleaning your room." He smiled. "You still have to do that. In return, however, when you choose to join in and be a family, you must be kind. You have been through a great deal of upheaval, but your cousins have been through even more. Please remember that we are all trying to do our best with the situation."

"Okay," said Amelia, wiping her eyes. She hadn't noticed herself starting to cry, and she willed the tears to stop. Crying was for eight-year-olds like Matthew.

"We love you, Amie," said her mother, kissing the top of her head. "We'll leave you to your book now, but if you need us, we're here for you."

Amelia nodded. She was so confused. She wanted to go home, but even if they could return, it would mean leaving the time-machine house. How could she like the house and hate living in it, all at once?

Thinking so hard gave her a headache; she was still a bit ill. But the answer came:

Because the house itself was the way to escape being stuck inside it. Her parents had basically just promised her they wouldn't come looking to disturb her.

"Horatio?" she called, doubtful.

"Miss Amelia," he answered, a shadow by the window. His dusty, heavy suit resolved into view, face becoming flesh.

"Take me somewhere else. Somewhere fun."

He snapped his fingers.

CHAPTER SEVEN

When Are We?

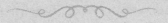

I N ALL THE BOOKS I'VE read," said Amelia, "time machines take you to famous places at important times. Like when that big boat sank or whatever."

Horatio laughed. "Those events are indeed interesting," he said, "but I will tell you a secret: They are only interesting *once.* You see them and then life returns to normal. But this, for example—why, there are a thousand tiny things to grab our attention. Have you ever seen anything like it?"

Amelia hadn't. She stared, agape at the scene in front of her. Horse-drawn carriages clattered over cobblestones; ladies in spectacularly fancy dresses wandered along under parasols to shield them from the drizzle that fell. The sky was a deep, dull gray. She'd made Horatio wait while she put on shoes this time, which was just as well, because the ground was utterly filthy. Filthy with what, exactly, was best not imagined. An ornate gas lamp a few feet above Amelia's head illuminated the grime. A gentleman across the street was riding the most *ridiculous* bicycle. The front wheel was nearly as tall as Amelia, while the back one was something a hamster might run around in.

"When are we?" Amelia asked, because Horatio had been pleased by her cleverness the first time. He nodded approvingly at her.

"The year 1882," he said. "More than one hundred years before you were born. Queen Victoria is on the throne, mourning her deceased husband. Your great-great-grandparents are younger than you are now. And though you have not asked, this is London. We may venture further afield next time, to other countries and other times, but I thought you might like to understand the words spoken around you, even if you can't speak back."

She had so many questions, each raising its little hand in her head to be called upon first. "I've never been to London," she said.

"Well, then, an excellent place to start. Shall we?"

She could ask things while they walked. Amelia kept close to Horatio's side as they ventured into a busy market, full of curious objects and ordinary ones that were curious too, because something as simple as an apple is a bizarre thing when your mind knows it's more than a century old. The apples shone red, and so did the clusters of garnets on rings that would surely now be called antiques. Silver-scaled fish and silver candlesticks, green cabbages and jade necklaces, they were all treasures. Voices buzzed, busier than a hive of bees, and despite what Horatio had said, Amelia understood perhaps half the words she caught. They seemed to have different words for everything: coins were *canary birds*; matches were *scratchers*. She could have listened to them all day.

Amelia stopped at a table to inspect a huge leather-bound book. A dictionary. Did it hold the same words as the one at home she prized so highly? She brushed her hand over the cover, felt the cracks with her fingertips. It was warm against her skin, unnaturally so, and only then did she realize she was cold, cold as she had been when they visited her old house in wintertime, though there was no snow on the ground here. If there had been, it would've turned quickly black with soot and muck.

"Why am I cold?" Amelia asked. Horatio tugged at the sleeves of his heavy suit. She'd never seen him wear anything else, even when he'd first shown himself in summer.

"Life creates warmth," he said simply. "It's been so long. . . . I'm sorry, Amelia; I should have thought to warn you. Dress warmly on all our coming adventures, all right? Right now, these people are alive around us, but we are not part of it, and so their heat doesn't touch us. On the other hand, this means we are not touching them, either." A wide smile on his face, Horatio winked and plucked the hat from the head of a passerby, tossed it up into the air. The man shrieked and grasped wildly for the hat. He caught it as it fell and looked this way and that for the source of the wind that had nearly stolen it.

Amelia laughed. "Okay," she said, another thought coming to her. "But if nothing is really touching us, why did I catch cold from my wet socks? That's not even an actual thing; it's just what people say. Mum tells me all the time to wrap up warm and dry or I'll catch cold," she continued, doing her very best impression of Mrs. Howling. "My socks weren't truly wet; I only thought they were."

"Aha," said Horatio, putting his fingers to his chin.

"Can I tell you . . . ? Yes. Because you convinced yourself it was true, my dear, if only for a short time. Thoughts that are not real thoughts, not *true* thoughts, that we tell our minds *are* true thoughts . . . well, they are like poison. And poison makes you ill, does it not?"

"Yes," said Amelia, "but isn't that just imagining things? Imagining things is fun."

"I do not remember imagination well," answered Horatio, turning his eyes from her to stare out across the throng. "But I should think that even when you are pretending an old sled to be a spaceship, you know you are doing so. Besides," he said, returning his gaze to her, "would you really wish to imagine yourself with wet socks?"

"Well, no." They were still standing beside the dictionary, the stallkeeper carrying on his business as if they weren't there—which, to him, they weren't.

"Can we take things back with us?" she asked. It wasn't the question she'd expected to choose next, but it was a necessary question.

"No," said Horatio, shaking his head. "I am sorry; that . . . is difficult. And if we did so, why, my poor house would fill up to the ceiling with treasures!"

"Can they ever see us?" Amelia waved her hand right in the face of the man behind the table. He smiled toothlessly at a woman who had arrived to stand beside Amelia. "'Ow can I help, madam?"

"Right now you are a shadow, just as you see me sometimes," said Horatio. "Most people aren't observant enough to notice that much. You are an unusual child, Miss Amelia."

Yes. She was special. Horatio had picked her, not Owen or Matthew. He hadn't waited to see what Lavender would be like when she was older.

Another loud question joined the chorus in Amelia's head, but she wouldn't ask that one. She'd never ask it. What mattered was that she had moved to the strange house and that Horatio had chosen her to share his secret. It was odd, however, to think that at this very moment she was as insubstantial as a cobweb to the milling crowd around her. She felt perfectly normal, and when she looked at the hand she had waved in front of the stallkeeper's face, it was as solid and real as it had ever been.

They left the market, slipping down a narrow street as crooked as a lie. Amelia was glad, for as interesting as the market had been, it was quieter here, thus easier to talk and be heard. "You haven't told me the third thing yet," she said as they passed an aproned woman hanging out what must have been a whole month's worth of laundry. All right, it wasn't technically a question, but it nonetheless demanded an answer. Horatio cocked his head to the side and stroked his chin.

"That is true," he said. "I wonder, are you ready to learn? It is not the simplest thing in the world or all of time to describe, and even less so to understand."

Annoyance flared once more in Amelia. How many times would she have to remind him how clever she was?

"I know you are clever, Amelia, I have said so many times. My reluctance has nothing to do with your intelligence, and everything to do with a question I have for *you*. You see, my dear, I did not reveal myself to you merely to keep you amused in my house, to which I know you wish you had never moved. I am not showing you its tricks to change your mind and make you love the home I built so carefully. I do hope you will come to love it as I do, but my reasons are much deeper than that. So, I will make you a bargain. Let us spend the rest of our time in this marvelous place seeing all of its wonders, and when we are finished, I will tell you what you must know, and ask you what I must ask. Would you like to see the queen?"

He was maddeningly just like her parents, making deals with her, but as with the other one, Amelia felt this was fair. He was right that this place—this *time*—was interesting, and she wanted to see all of it.

As their shadow selves they stepped between the bars of the gates around the palace and crept, unnoticed, into the room where the queen sat by a high window. Uniformed girls stood at the edges of the room, surely waiting to be called upon if their mistress needed anything. Someone else was there too, standing by a large box on a stand with three legs. It took Amelia a moment to work out what it was, and she was determined to work it out alone, without asking Horatio. He had something he wanted from her, and it wouldn't do to make him think she was an idiot.

It was a camera. She knew what a camera was, of course. Her parents had always taken pictures of her—though not, now she came to think of it, since they had arrived at her cousins' house, the calendar house—but their cameras didn't look anything like this one.

"Stay still, Your Majesty, if you please," said the man behind it.

"What do you think I'm doing?" she retorted. Her black dress made her wide face look very pale. The crown on her head caught the light, a thousand diamond sparkles.

"Of course, Your Majesty."

Horatio smiled at Amelia. "One of the most surprising things," he said, "is learning that even queens are much like the rest of us. I have seen more than my fair share, and believe me, they are all perfectly ordinary people. If slightly murderous, on occasion."

"Wh-what?" asked Amelia.

"Not this one," he assured her. "But in the earlier days, the barbarian kings, well . . . We may visit them at some point, if you like."

She did like. She could go anywhere now, anywhere in all of time or space. And she thought she understood, a bit, how the time thing worked. She didn't know exactly how Horatio achieved it, but going back and forth in time was, at least, a concept she could get her head around.

"How come we can go anywhere in the world?" she asked. "Wouldn't it make more sense if we could just visit the house at different times? How can we move places, too?"

Horatio shook his head. "What did we agree about questions, Amelia? Later."

They left the queen to her portrait, visited a museum and a library and a dressmaker and a hospital. That was *gruesome*. Amelia hadn't ever been to London before, but she had been to a hospital to get her tonsils out, and she was fairly certain she would have remembered if they had come at her with any of those long, curved hooks. They *had* put her to sleep, however, so maybe she wouldn't have remembered.

Either way, Amelia didn't think being a doctor was in her future, the future she had over a century from now. She was clever enough, but blood was disgusting.

Outside, on the steps of the hospital, Horatio drew a watch on a long chain from a pocket on his vest. That was something else Amelia had never seen—not just his watch, but any one such as that. She craned her neck to get a proper look at it, but Horatio angled the face away from her so she couldn't see.

"It is time for us to return, Miss Amelia. Which means it is time for me to ask you my question."

"All right," she said, curious, but disappointed that they couldn't stay in the past forever.

Another smile twitched Horatio's lips. "You don't want to leave," he said. "But that is exactly what I wish to ask of you. Would you like the ability to do this forever? To travel as I do? To live outside of time, as I do? The time has come for me to choose an apprentice, and I have chosen you. I can teach you all I know. I can make you into what I am."

• • •

Horatio was gone. Amelia sat at the table with her parents and cousins, pushing food around her plate. It had been a whole day since she'd seen him, a day of little food and little sleep as his request spun around her head, bouncing off all her thoughts like a rubber ball that would never stay still.

It didn't escape her that he had asked his question without answering many of hers, even at the end, which he'd promised. She suspected he'd done this on purpose, stunning her into silence and leaving her in her uncle's office on this side of the twenty-fourth door. If that had been his plan all along, it had certainly worked.

Well. Amelia was excellent at making plans too. She wouldn't give him an answer until he'd told her everything she wanted to know. And that wouldn't be difficult, since she didn't know what the answer would be.

Lavender had food all over her face. The boys were squabbling over who could fit more spaghetti in their mouths—quietly, so Mr. and Mrs. Howling didn't notice as they talked about boring things like work and who would do the shopping this week. Mrs. Howling would be returning to work when Amelia, Owen, and Matthew began school in a few days, doing her job from the computer she had set up in the conservatory while Lavender played at her feet.

It was all so *ordinary,* so *boring.* What Horatio had shown her was extraordinary and exciting, and he had shown it only to her, not to Owen or Matthew or Lavender. She was the special one.

But what would happen if she said yes? She couldn't very well just go missing; as busy and preoccupied as her parents were with her cousins and work and everything else, she was reasonably sure—she *hoped*—that they would notice if one day she simply wasn't around anymore at all. They'd said they would leave her alone except for suppertimes; she still had to turn up for those. Mum wouldn't drive off to the school without Amelia in the car, and neither parent would shrug and kiss her pillow good night if she wasn't in her bed.

"May I please be excused?" Amelia asked.

Her mother set down her fork and eyed Amelia's plate. "Are you still ill?" asked Mrs. Howling. "You've hardly touched your food."

"Can I finish it?" asked Owen.

Amelia pushed her plate over to him. "I'm fine," she said. "I'm just excited about school. I want to go organize the things you bought me."

"Oh," said Mrs. Howling, relieved. This was the Amelia she knew. "Of course, darling. If you get hungry before bed, come and get a snack. I'll make sure there's something."

"I will. Thanks, Mum." Amelia pushed her chair back and left the kitchen through the door to the conservatory. She wanted to smell the petrichor. Horatio was right, the *spring* of the house was everywhere on this floor, but he was also right that it was strongest here. Spring here, winter in the cellar, summer in the bedrooms, autumn in the attic with its curiously shaped fifty-second window.

She stood in the middle of the conservatory, this green, open space made of glass. She was counting. In her head she went through the rest of the house. Twelve rooms and seven fireplaces, four floors and— she had checked these earlier—sixty stairs with twenty-four railings going up each staircase. Twenty-four doors, fifty-two windows, probably other numbers she hadn't thought of yet, all making up this house of months and years and days and hours.

At least one thing didn't fit; there were supposedly three hundred sixty-five trees, they were outside the house itself. One house, one year, but still there should really be something indoors to mark each day of it. Asking Horatio, if she could get him to answer, would be easier than counting all the tiles in the kitchen and bathrooms put together, or whatever else it might be.

Quietly, because Mum and Dad thought she'd gone several minutes ago, Amelia went up to her room. The pile of school supplies sat on her dresser, not exactly what Amelia would have chosen for herself, if she'd had the chance. Pink wasn't her favorite color. Maybe there hadn't been much of a selection, or maybe Mum had been too busy with Lavender and the boys.

She left the pile where it was and went to her uncle's office. The book with the picture of the house in it was on his desk; the twenty-fourth door was closed fast against the wall.

Hmmm. The first time she'd seen it and opened it, there'd been a brick wall behind, but that was before she'd known what the door could do, what it could hold on the other side. The rest of the world and all of time. Would it be different now?

No.

Her hand still gripped the knob as she stared in disappointment at the bricks. She wanted to be able to do what Horatio could do. Escape through the doorway to anywhere she wanted to go, whenever she wanted to be there. Get away from this house full of busy parents and annoying cousins.

"You lied," came Owen's voice. "I should tell on you."

"They wouldn't believe you," said Amelia, turning to glare at him. "By the time they got here, I'd be in my room. Besides, I was only . . ."

She couldn't—wouldn't—tell him what she'd been trying to do, so she stopped and let the words hang there.

Owen scowled back at her. "I don't care if your mum did say you could come in here. It's *my* dad's office, and I don't want you to."

Amelia still wasn't cruel enough to say what she'd nearly said the first time they'd argued about this room, even though now it would be for a different reason. It wasn't his father's office, because it was Horatio's house; he only let them live here.

Needed them to live here.

It could be her house, more than Owen's or Matthew's or Lavender's. She already knew its secret.

Yes.

CHAPTER EIGHT

A Most Unusual Meal

THERE WERE DIFFERENT KINDS OF years. A year could begin on the first of January, with snow on the ground and an empty nail hammered into the wall, waiting for the new calendar to replace the old. It could begin on a birthday morning, with one more candle on a cake than there had been twelve months before. Or it could begin like this.

Amelia stood beside her mother's car, staring at the outside of her new school, which looked nothing like her old school, nervous butterflies made of cornflakes fluttering in her belly. Mrs. Frenkel wouldn't be in there, and neither would Isabelle. The only familiar faces would be Owen's and Matthew's, and she didn't want to see those. She clutched her bag tighter and tilted her head to let Mum kiss her cheek.

"Amelia, are you sure you don't want me to come in with you since it's your first day here? I can get Lavender out of her seat."

"No, thank you," said Amelia. She could figure it out on her own. Horatio probably wasn't watching her now, but just in case, she didn't want him to think he'd made a mistake, choosing her, if she needed her mum to hold her hand through anything scary.

"All right," said Mrs. Howling. "Have a good day, everyone. I'll be back to pick you up later." She climbed back into the car and the engine revved to life.

"Follow me," said Owen, turning away and starting up the path to the front doors.

"Why?"

"Because we're in the same class, of course."

The butterflies became huge, angry birds instead, full of claws and beaks. How had she not thought of that? Owen was only a week older than she was, a fact that had apparently greatly pleased her mum and her aunt when they'd both found out they were expecting children. Then Amelia's aunt and uncle had moved away, and she and Owen hadn't grown up as friends as their mothers had thought they might. They'd gotten along all right whenever they'd seen each other, but it was easy to get along with someone who'd be leaving you alone soon.

They were not friends now. Amelia stomped along behind Owen and Matthew, into the school and down a hallway. As in her old school, the walls were covered with artwork and posters telling the students what to do, and teachers stood in doorways calling, "Don't run," in bossy voices. Amelia didn't mind teachers being bossy; they were supposed to be, and she had always done what she was told. She greatly minded Owen being bossy, though, so when he ordered her into the next classroom, she stuck her tongue out at his back.

"None of that," said a woman with a face like a squeezed lemon and yellow hair to match. "Owen, it's so good to see you again. How are you?"

"I'm all right, Mrs. Murdoch, thank you."

"I was so sorry to hear, dear," she said, eyes full of sympathy. "Please come to me if there's anything you need."

Owen nodded. "That's my cousin, Amelia," he said, jerking his thumb over his shoulder. The sympathy disappeared as Mrs. Murdoch turned her gaze once more upon Amelia.

"Yes," she said, "I heard. Welcome, Miss Howling. I trust you will behave in my class?"

"Of course," Amelia said sweetly, trying to show that she was a good student who always did her schoolwork on time and never whispered in the middle of a lesson. She'd never had a teacher dislike her before, and Mrs. Murdoch wouldn't be the first. Which didn't mean Amelia had to like *her*.

Mrs. Murdoch smiled so stiffly the temperature around Amelia dropped. She followed Owen inside and found an empty desk at the back of the room, tucking her bag neatly under it so there was scarcely enough room for her feet. Most of the other desks were full, boys and girls unpacking pencils and chattering to their friends after a long summer. One or two looked like kids Amelia might want to be friends with, but she didn't know what to say. She and Isabelle had just always been friends, growing up as close as sisters, and Isabelle had done a good job of finding anyone else they needed for their adventures during recess. *Finding* in that case meaning Isabelle simply telling people what to do. She would probably be a teacher when she grew up.

Contrary to what anyone would likely think, the first day of school was not Amelia's favorite, even at her old school. It was all too full of introductions and instructions; they didn't actually learn anything. This was no different, and Amelia dutifully stood to say her name when asked, and wrote her name on sticky labels on the covers of battered schoolbooks, and let herself be swept up in the rush for lunch.

She ate alone. She'd never eaten a school lunch alone. On the days Isabelle had been home sick with a cold or, for two horrible weeks, chicken pox, there were others Amelia knew. Owen invited her to sit with his friends, but she knew he didn't really mean it, and she was still angry. Stuck in the house with him for half the summer, now stuck with him at school, too. Matthew was across the room, but Amelia would rather have eaten a plate of slugs for lunch than spent an hour with a bunch of younger kids.

For that matter she would rather have eaten a plate of slugs, full stop. The food had been better at her old school. Everything had been better at her old school, just as everything had been better at her old house.

Except . . .

Except Horatio. Her old house hadn't been a magic house, with a magic shadow-man living in it.

When Mrs. Howling fetched them from school after the last lesson, which couldn't be called a lesson, in Amelia's opinion, she climbed into the car beside Lavender and told her mother that the first day had been fine. Of course Mum wanted to know whether she'd made any friends or learned anything interesting. Amelia shrugged and watched as her mother tried to smile while she asked Owen and Matthew how *their* first days had been.

She had no schoolwork to do yet, so she shut herself in the library the moment they got back, curling up in her favorite chair with the book Matthew had tried to take from her. It wasn't a very good book—she'd made a bad choice from the thousands on the shelves—but that wasn't the point. She was reading it; she wanted to finish it.

And she hoped Horatio might come if she was alone. She'd kept her shoes on, just in case. The hours stretched until supper, when Amelia reluctantly dragged herself to the table and sat down in front of a lamb chop. Her stomach growled at the sight; she hadn't eaten much at dinner yesterday, hardly any of the disgusting school lunch today. She wolfed it down, and potatoes, and the pile of broccoli, too, which made her father's eyebrows rise almost all the way into his hair. He, too, asked Amelia how her day was, as if Mum hadn't already told him what she'd said.

"It was all right," she said, setting down her fork. "It's just that I don't know anyone there, and they never actually teach anything on the first day. Except I did learn where the fire exits are." Hardly as interesting as history or English.

"The first day can be like that," Dad agreed. "But you know Owen and Matthew; it isn't true that you don't know anyone."

"They have their own friends," said Amelia. "Owen did introduce me to our teacher, though. Thank you, Owen."

"No problem," said Owen around a mouthful of potato. Disgusting. She waited for one of her parents to tell him not to speak with his mouth full. Neither did. Mrs. Howling smiled instead at Amelia for being nice at the table, and gave her an extra scoop of ice cream when it was time for dessert.

"May I take it upstairs with me?" Amelia asked. Mr. Howling sighed, but nodded.

When she was excused, Amelia ran upstairs so she would be out of everyone's earshot when she called for Horatio. He hadn't come to her, so she would make him. Shout and scream if she had to, and beat on the twenty-fourth door with her fists. She put the bowl of ice cream on her uncle's desk and ran to the door.

"I hardly think that's necessary," Horatio said as she raised her hand over the wood. "I am right here."

"Oh," said Amelia as he stepped from the shadows. "Hello."

"Hello, Miss Amelia. Have you had a good day?"

Amelia frowned. "I don't want to talk about my day," she said.

"As you wish. Well, then. I wondered if you would like to accompany me to a rather special dinner."

"I've already eaten. But I want to come!" she insisted as Horatio frowned.

"Excellent."

"And I want you to answer my questions."

"I will." Horatio stepped over to join Amelia at the door. "You have my word." He placed his hand on the doorknob and turned it, a creaking of bone and hinge.

"Where are we?" she asked, forgetting herself and what Horatio thought was clever.

"I told you: at a very special dinner."

"All right." Amelia huffed. "*When* are we?"

"Aha." Horatio began to lead the way across the lush grass that now spread out before them. It was dark, but the lights of a house ahead shone with life. "A time," he said, "outside of time."

Candles in brackets on stone walls lit a long table covered in midnight-blue silk. Every chair, except one, was filled. Just as Amelia noticed this from her spot half hidden behind Horatio, the table's occupants, perhaps twenty people, noticed *them*.

"Horatio!" they cried.

"And is this the girl?" asked an elegant woman in an old-fashioned, plum-colored dress, a matching hat dipping low over one eye. "Wonderful. Amelia, is it?"

"Y-yes," said Amelia, stepping out into full view. "Good evening."

"Manners," said the woman. "I approve. Well done, Horatio. Felix, get the girl a chair."

The youngest person at the table—a man who still must have been more than twice Amelia's age—leaped up and dashed from the room, returning a moment later with a stool covered in a fancy, bumpy kind of fabric. *Brocade,* Amelia thought, remembering her dictionary. He placed it beside the remaining empty place, which was clearly Horatio's. "There you are, Madame Roseline."

"Thank you, Felix. Please, Amelia, do sit down."

With a glance at Horatio, who nodded, Amelia sat carefully on the stool and cast her eyes up and down the table. Madame Roseline was one of those beautiful, rare women who could be anywhere between thirty and eighty. Amber earrings dangled from her ears.

Felix was young. The others covered the spectrum of age, with Horatio somewhere in the middle, but it occurred to Amelia as she examined their faces that what they looked like might not mean anything. A time outside of time, and Horatio was certainly older than he looked, if indeed he had built the house. According to the book in her uncle's office, the calendar house had been built in built in 1882.

Amelia's eyes widened. Horatio had taken her to 1882. Had he been there, in London, while they were? Had there been two Horatios in that marketplace? Once again she couldn't ask him about this, for the others were starting to introduce themselves, nodding at Amelia as they went up and down the table, giving their names.

"It's very nice to meet you all," she said.

Madame Roseline picked up her knife and fork. "Horatio tells us he has chosen you as his apprentice, that you will become one of us."

So, they *were* all like Horatio. She had guessed this, because why else would she be here? "Yes," said Amelia. "I think so, yes. Do you all have special houses of your own?" Horatio hadn't answered so many of her questions, and she hadn't asked half the ones she wanted to, but maybe the rest of them would tell her what he hadn't.

"Some of us." Madame Roseline laughed, a sound richer than butter or diamonds. "Klaus over there let his ambitions get the better of him. He has a castle."

"And a fine castle it is, too," retorted Klaus, tucking a napkin into his chin. He, too, wore an amber ring. Perhaps it was like a badge of some kind, and all the shadow-people wore the stone. "It works, that's all that matters."

Works. The castle let Klaus travel through time, as the house let Horatio. Amelia looked back at all the faces, one by one, trying to imagine what type of home each one had built. The plump, happy woman at the far end would have a cottage with a thatched roof, perhaps, and Felix a town house in the middle of a city.

She was so busy with this game that it took her much longer than it should have to realize something extremely odd, as if everything Horatio had done or shown her up to this point hadn't been odd enough. Dropping her eyes, Amelia watched not their faces, but their plates, listening to the sounds of chewing and enjoyment, the clanking of silver on the finest bone china. As they ate, they spoke of their travels, the things they had seen. Which, as Amelia knew, was what people did when they returned from being away. More than once she had sat at the dinner table in her old house, crowded together with her parents and their friends as they talked about their latest holidays.

On those occasions, however, the plates had always been full of food.

"Horatio?" she whispered, tugging on his dusty sleeve. He paused in his conversation with the man on his other side to look at her.

"Yes, my dear?"

"Do they . . . Do they know they aren't eating anything?"

But even as she asked, Horatio had taken a forkful of air from his plate and put it in his mouth, jaws working as if he were chewing the juiciest steak.

He did not laugh at her. "When you are one of us, Amelia, you will see what we are eating. You may be here because I have brought you, as you may visit all the times in the world if I take you there, but you are still . . . human. There are things you won't be able to see, or do, quite yet."

It was his use of the word *human* that sent a thrill of fear through Amelia. If she became what he wanted her to be, one of them who sat in this room, she would no longer be human.

She would be *special*. She would be a shadow-woman.

Or possibly . . . a shadow-girl. "If I become one of you, will I be ten forever?"

Again he didn't laugh. "No. To begin with, you will not be ready for a while yet. There is more I must teach you, more I must show you. The process will not be fully complete until you have completed construction of a calendar house of your own, though you will be able to travel through time long before that. Apart from that, you will age until the last person who remembers you passes away. That is why some of us appear young, and some old, and some in the middle. Felix, for example, his parents died when he was scarcely an adult, and he had no other family, no friends."

Amelia glanced at Felix. How sad it must be, to be forgotten, but he was laughing at a joke she hadn't heard. She caught Madame Roseline's eye, and the woman set down an empty wineglass.

"You must think us rude, Amelia," said Madame Roseline. "I promise we are not; it is merely that we remember how overwhelming this can be. It is better to let you get used to everything and speak when you wish. If you are ready, I would dearly love to hear more about you than what Horatio has already told us."

It felt a bit as if Amelia had traveled back in time a few hours, to when she was standing at her desk in her new classroom. It was, indeed, a day of introductions. But she told Madame Roseline, and the others who had stopped to listen, all about her little house on its hill, and about moving to live with her cousins, and that of all the rooms in the calendar house she liked the library best. Or she had, until Horatio had taught her the secret of the twenty-fourth door.

"Does everyone in all your houses stop dreaming too?" Amelia asked next. Felix dropped his fork, but Horatio began to juggle his—and his knife—over his empty plate.

"Dreams waste . . . energy, my dear. We want you all to save your energy for enjoying our houses that we took such care to build," Horatio said. The cutlery flashed, catching the candlelight. "Next question?"

"I understand how the house lets us move in time—I mean, all right, I don't understand it at all, but it does; I know it does. How can it let us move to other places, too? That part makes no sense."

Farther down the table Klaus laughed. "It makes all the sense in the world, young Amelia, but you probably haven't learned this yet. From a scientific perspective, you see, time and space are precisely the same thing. To move in one is to move in the other. Horatio, you shall have to take the girl to one of Einstein's lectures."

Einstein. Amelia had heard of him.

"You like words, details. You see the spin of things, how everything around us has meaning and importance. And you are more lonely now than you were when you were an only child." Madame Roseline turned her gaze on Horatio. "An excellent choice, old friend. We would be glad to have her."

Horatio smiled, clearly very pleased. He drew his watch from his pocket and angled the face away from Amelia. "I am elated you think so, but we must go."

"We must all go," Madame Roseline agreed, rising. "Do join us again, Amelia."

They had come down a corridor of closed doors when they arrived, and they left the same way, out the front door and across the lush grass. When Horatio stopped, Amelia couldn't tell what made this spot better than any other for Horatio to snap his fingers. Another door, a familiar door, appeared, and he opened it. "I bid you good night here," he said, ushering Amelia back into her uncle's office. "I will fetch you again soon."

"Wait—" said Amelia, but he had gone, melted into the shadows. She should be used to this by now. Head spinning, Amelia crossed the room to go to her own, and froze, staring at her uncle's desk.

When Horatio had taken her to see her house that wasn't hers anymore, or to the London of the past, she had thought he'd brought her home before her parents had a chance to notice she was missing. That was why he checked his pocket watch.

That couldn't be right. She picked up the spoon in the bowl.

The ice cream hadn't melted.

CHAPTER NINE

Swords & Secrets

BOTH THINGS COULD BE TRUE. Amelia sat in class, pretending to work on her multiplication. Horatio had said that the dinner was outside of time, so perhaps that was why the ice cream hadn't melted. The other places they had gone weren't outside of time, just at different times, so maybe for those he had been worried that her parents would begin to miss her. She hadn't thought to check what the clocks said before they left.

Not that clocks were trustworthy things. The one on the wall of the classroom was moving far too slowly; she *must* have been sitting here for more than twenty minutes. A few feet away, Owen's head was bent over his paper; his pencil was scribbling furiously. Hmph. Math was not Amelia's favorite subject, but she wasn't about to let Owen be better than her at anything. Quickly she wrote down all the answers, counting on her fingers under the desk, where no one could see. Then she went back to thinking about Horatio and Madame Roseline and the strange dinner where the plates had been bare and the glasses empty but everyone had eaten and drunk.

But they hadn't been bare or empty to Horatio and the others. Amelia wanted to eat what they ate, drink what they drank, do what they did.

The final bell rang far too many hours later. Amelia was packing her books away when another girl— Amelia couldn't remember her name—stopped beside her desk.

"I'm having a birthday party on Saturday," she said. "Mum said to give you an invitation." The girl dropped a folded card on the desk, a cartoon mouse on the front. Christina, that was her name.

"Oh," said Amelia. "Um. Thank you. I might be busy that day, though." She hoped she would be busy adventuring somewhere with Horatio.

"That's all right. See you," said Christina, sauntering away. Amelia stuffed the invitation into the bottom of her bag and ran from the school to the car, the bag banging painfully against her ribs, and waited even more painfully for Owen and Matthew to hurry up. They were so slow, lingering there by the doors, chatting to their friends. Amelia answered her mother's questions about how her day had been without really listening to them. It was only school, and even though it had been just a few months earlier, she could barely remember the time when school had been the best, most exciting part of her day.

School was always the same place, the same time. Behind the twenty-fourth door could be anything, anywhere. Amelia was the first to jump from the car when it stopped at the top of the long drive, the first to run through the front door her mother hadn't bothered to lock. Perhaps she thought she didn't need to, the house being so far away from everything else.

Perhaps—although Mrs. Howling couldn't possibly know this—Horatio protected the house and made sure no terrible harm came to it or inside it. And maybe that protection only stretched to the outer edge of the forest, because he hadn't been able to stop what had happened to Amelia's aunt and uncle.

"Amelia!" her mother called when Amelia was halfway up the precisely numbered staircase with its exact

number of railings running from the smooth oak bannister. "Do you want a snack?"

"No, thanks! I'm going to do my homework."

"Oh, all right, then. Come down for supper."

"Yes, Mum."

Amelia dropped her bag on her bed and left it there
without opening it. Closing her bedroom door behind
her, so that any nosy cousins or mothers who wandered
past would simply think she was inside, she went into
the office and stood at the door in the wall. "Horatio?"
she called.

"Good afternoon, Amelia."

She was expecting him, had called for him, and still
it was a tiny bit of a surprise when he stepped from the
shadows and became a man, because she couldn't be
certain, until he did, that he would come at all.

"I read a book once," she said. "Well, I've read lots
of books, but I read one with knights and castles and
kings and queens in it. I want to go there." Horatio
came closer. The lines on his face appeared deeper in
the gloom. "Do you sleep?" she asked.

"Not in the way you assume," he said, reaching for
the door handle. "I am tired, Amelia, and so I will need
your help if we are to do this. I cannot take you to a
fictional place, of course, so it will not be entirely like

your book. I can, however, provide what I think you're after. Are you dressed warmly enough?"

Amelia barely heard anything except "help." Excitement bubbled in her tummy. This was it, wasn't it? This was when he would begin to teach her what he knew, start teaching her how to be like him, or Madame Roseline, or Felix. "What can I do?"

"I need you to think of a memory," he said. "Any memory will do, the more detailed the better."

A million pictures flipped through Amelia's mind like the pages of a photograph album. Every time she decided, she suddenly thought of a better one. She shut her eyes, concentrating. The first time she'd gone through the door with Horatio, he'd taken her to her old house at Christmas, the house that wasn't hers anymore. But it had been. The image of a turkey, roasted golden and delicious on a table decked with holly and candles, pushed itself in front of all the others. The last one in that house, though she hadn't known then it would be the last one. That had been an excellent day; she'd woken up when it was still dark, despite staying up late listening for the sound of reindeer hooves she didn't completely believe in anymore. Her parents were still asleep, but she was always allowed to go to the living room and open her stocking. The stack of presents under the tree waited until everyone was awake, and her mother made hot chocolate to drink while they were opened and the floor became a mess of boxes and bright, glossy wrapping paper. She'd played with her new toys and read her new books until the scent of food became overwhelming in the little house. Surrounding the turkey were bowls of mashed potatoes and stuffing and green beans.

She felt Horatio take her hand, heard him inhale deeply and swallow. She remembered going outside, stuffed to bursting with the excellent Christmas dinner, to scrape snow from the bushes in the garden and form snowballs with her gloved hands. Isabelle and her parents had come out to join in the fight, continued until everyone was gasping in the cold air.

"Well done," said Horatio. "Open your eyes, Miss Amelia."

"Why did I do that?" she asked before obeying.

"A distraction," he said easily. "To trick the mind. Now open your eyes."

She did, and gasped just as she'd done in her memory. The castle before them was whole, every stone in place, not the ruins to which her parents had occasionally taken her on days out at the weekends. There was an actual drawbridge, a moat of dark, muddy water.

People in strange clothing bustled about, with curious hairstyles or coverings on their heads, and a great noise came from somewhere behind Amelia. The sound of cheering.

"What was that?" Amelia turned. The castle sat atop a hill. At the bottom, where the ground flattened out, an arena of sorts had been built from thick wooden planks, festooned in massive embroidered tapestries that fluttered in the breeze. The stands were full of people, all chattering and watching the empty space in the middle.

"I believe we have arrived to see the games," said Horatio.

"Games, like at school?"

"In a manner of speaking," said Horatio mysteriously. "Remember your book, Amelia. Things were different . . . now."

They moved toward the roar of people and, as they neared, the thundering sound of what could only be horses. Definitely not reindeer.

Unseen, Amelia and Horatio climbed the creaking steps into the stands, Amelia leading the way. Horatio moved slowly, following her. He still seemed tired, but when she glanced over her shoulder, he was smiling, the creases around his mouth deep with good humor. When they reached the top, Amelia looked up and down the packed rows for a place to sit, finding nowhere. It seemed almost everyone from the castle, and people from miles around, must have come for these mysterious games. It was a nice day for it, the sun shining, and were it not for the strangeness of the clothing and the pristine castle looming from the hill, Amelia could have been anywhere, any*when*. It wasn't the first time she'd felt that; in fact, now that she thought about it, she'd felt that way in the old London, too, with people bustling about, going on with their lives. It had never occurred to her before that people were basically the same wherever, whenever, they lived. Nearby, two well-dressed ladies were complimenting each other's gowns, and while the gowns in question were a great deal longer and more intricate than anything in Mum's closet, the conversation was not very much different from ones Mrs. Howling used to have with Isabelle's mum, the two women complimenting each other on jumpers or shoes or handbags. They would talk about their jobs, too, of course, and Amelia imagined that was one thing that *was* different; she remembered her book, that the ladies in it had mostly sat around sewing and waiting for the men to come home.

That sounded *boring*, so it was good some things had changed.

The crowd went silent, suddenly, as if someone had just turned off the sound on the world. Amelia held her breath as Horatio took her hand and led her to a little gap between the front row of crude wooden benches and the equally crude railing meant to stop anyone from toppling over into the arena. Her eyes tried to go in separate directions when they caught sight of the horses approaching the field from opposite sides. Her mouth dropped open, and she tugged the side of Horatio's dusty jacket. One horse was an enormous beast, black and shiny as the chunk of obsidian on Amelia's dresser, a memory from a museum gift shop after she'd spent hours looking at the rocks. Steam billowed from its nostrils as it snorted and stomped, impatient. It was draped in rich red fabrics, and the effect was an angry kind of beautiful, with the gleaming black of the animal and the silver of the armor on the man in the saddle. The man—Amelia was sure it was a man, though a mask obscured his face—raised a long spear thing. Around her the audience erupted in cheers.

"What's that called?" she whispered to Horatio.

"You and your words. That, my dear, is called a lance. We are here for the joust."

The other rider raised his lance in response, and the cheering swelled from loud to louder. His armor was the same silvery steel, but his horse was the color of a perfect autumn chestnut, swathed in deep purple. Directly across from Amelia, far on the other side of the arena, a man who could only be a king—because the crown on his head was a dead giveaway—stood and gestured to the men on horseback, who bowed deeply, a difficult trick on a horse; then he waved at the people around him, sleeves of the same purple flapping with the movement. He opened his mouth, and though he spoke loud enough to hear, Amelia could make out only a few of the words. His accent was thick, forming itself around unrecognizable syllables.

"What's he saying? Aren't we still in England?"

Horatio smiled. "We are, but languages change over time, Amelia. People did not speak then the way you do. He is welcoming his loyal subjects to the games, and explaining the rules."

"What are the rules?"

"In essence, that the one who stays on his horse wins. Everybody already knows this, but it is part of the ceremony."

It was Amelia's turn to smile. That was simple enough. Like in hide-and-seek, where the winner was the person to stay hidden the longest.

The king took his seat once more, and another silence fell, an expectant silence. Just when Amelia thought neither she nor anyone else in the crowd could wait one second longer, a bell rang, echoing everywhere, bouncing off the walls of the castle above and the hilltops in the distance.

The black horse reared, red fabric rippling like blood from a cut finger. It lunged forward as the chestnut one kicked its hind legs and ran to meet it in the center of the rectangle of dirt, the purple knight raising his lance to take aim at the chest of the other. A thrust, a miss, a cry of disappointment from the gathered spectators. Amelia's hand flew from Horatio's jacket to her mouth, covering her tiny scream. Beside her, Horatio joined in the clapping and jeering as the knights circled their mounts and aimed for each other a second time. He whistled loudly, all traces of his earlier, obvious tiredness gone now, and a thrill of fear that he would be heard shot through Amelia. She tore her eyes from the joust; the people around them were paying no attention. Indeed the grubby, apple-faced woman directly behind Amelia was watching right *through* her, eyes bright with excitement and stubby fingers at her lips. As Amelia whipped her head back to the game, the woman produced an ear-piercing whistle.

The horses charged again. The black one was several inches taller, wider at the shoulders, hooves the size of dinner plates carving circles in the soil, but the chestnut one was lighter, nimble on slender legs. Graceful, it danced along the earth, seeming to obey its rider's thoughts as much as his whip. For one desperate instant it looked as if they would race right past each other, until the purple knight swung his arm in a graceful arc and the tip of his lance caught the red one square in the chest. The great black horse reared, and the knight flew from its back in a much less graceful arc, crashing to the ground, sending up a spray of soil. Immense cheers and whoops erupted all around; even Horatio was clapping.

"Is he all right?" Amelia asked, but even as she did so, the fallen knight stood, obviously dazed, to give the king a stumbling bow. The king beckoned to him. "He's not about to be beheaded for losing, is he?"

"No." Horatio chuckled. "This is simply for fun, and for the competitors to earn prizes. Of course, the skills they display here are valued in battle, too. We cannot stay too much longer, Amelia. Would you like to continue watching, or would you like to see some more of the castle before we must leave?"

Amelia frowned. She wanted to do both. "Why do we have to leave at all? I saw the ice cream."

"Ice cream?" Horatio asked, wrinkles shifting into confusion.

"When you took me to meet the others, I left a bowl of ice cream in the house, and when I came back, it hadn't melted at all."

"Come." Horatio took her hand again and moved to leave the arena, but Amelia pulled away.

"No. You keep not answering my questions and then I forget to ask them again. I want to know."

"I was going to answer," he said, his shoulders slumping. Amelia wasn't quite sure she believed him. "I can do it right here, if you insist."

"I insist."

Horatio's lips moved, but barely any sound came out. Amelia thought he might have said *clever girl.* He'd called her that before, and she *was* clever. Sometimes cleverness meant asking the right questions and stomping her foot until she found out what she wanted to know. "You are right," he said. "When we are on our travels, no time passes in the world you know. It is as if we have hit pause on one of those television contraptions humans have become so fond of." Suddenly the tiredness Amelia had noticed before returned to Horatio's dark eyes. "Nonetheless, we can't leave that world paused forever. We will run out of time."

"What do you mean? You control time. Your house does. Your name even means 'time.' I looked it up."

"Why am I not surprised?" His mouth quirked into a smile. "Naturally you did. How do I explain this? I've never tried before. All right. You awake in the morning and you have breakfast, yes?"

"If my cousins haven't eaten all the pancakes."

"Indeed. Well, after you've eaten breakfast, you have enough energy to do all the things you need to do in the morning, but then before long you get hungry again, don't you?"

"You're saying you get hungry . . . for time?"

"A little like that, yes."

In the arena two new horses, one yellow and one gray, with two new knights atop them, were preparing to run at each other. This time the knights held swords. Amelia folded her arms across her chest and thought. "Was that what you were eating at dinner? Was that why I couldn't see it?"

"That is the easiest way to explain it, yes."

"Oh. What does it taste like?"

"Sometimes, I suppose, it tastes like pancakes." A

hint of the twinkle came back to Horatio's eyes. "Let us go explore, and next time I shall do what I can to keep us on our adventure for longer; how's that?"

This time Amelia let him take her from the stands, and she followed him back up to the castle.

CHAPTER TEN

A Visitor Arrives

SOMETHING WAS VERY WRONG WITH Mr. and Mrs. Howling.

For starters, her father hadn't left for work yet, and it was only Friday. *Tomorrow* he'd be home all day. Usually he kissed Amelia good-bye while she was in the middle of breakfast, but she'd already brushed her teeth and put her schoolbooks into her bag and he was still milling around the kitchen, sipping tea from his favorite mug and winking at Amelia's mother. And her mother kept winking back! It was obvious they had a secret of some kind; this sort of behavior was usually reserved for Amelia's birthday, which wasn't for months yet. She didn't think it was any of her cousins' birthdays either, though she couldn't remember when Matthew's or Lavender's were. And they kept looking at Amelia.

She tied the last bow in her shoelace and stood, staring at both of them. "All right," she said. "You two are up to something. Why hasn't Dad gone to work yet?"

"We don't know what you mean," said Mrs. Howling, eyes wide with innocence.

"I have an important appointment today," said Mr. Howling.

Amelia stomped her foot. "What's going on?" Matthew asked, walking into the kitchen.

"They're being *parents*," said Amelia.

"Oh. Um," said Matthew. Mr. Howling roared with laughter, and Mrs. Howling held up her hands.

"All right, all right. Amelia, we'll have a surprise for you this weekend."

Ohhhh. It all made sense now. They used to do this kind of thing sometimes, surprise her with a trip away to a zoo or museum or the seaside. Excitement rose in her throat and stopped on her tongue. Horatio had promised her more adventures this weekend, good ones. They'd better be good; he hadn't taken her anywhere in quite a while now, and she was getting more and more annoyed about it. He was busy, he said on the occasions he'd come to say hello. He was going to have a big surprise for her soon. On the other hand, she'd have Mum and Dad to herself again if *they* took her someplace.

"Where are we going?" she asked. "Who will look after Owen and Matthew and Lavender?"

Her parents exchanged glances, their smiles a little muted now. "We're not going anywhere, sweetheart, though we might perhaps go away somewhere soon, *all* of us."

Amelia barely heard the second part. If they weren't going anywhere, she could still adventure with Horatio. Excellent.

"Okay," she said cheerfully. "So what's the surprise?"

"You'll see it later. Time to go to school."

The old Amelia would have spent all day wondering what the surprise was, although the old Amelia also would've felt guilty for not paying attention to her teachers. The old Amelia had stayed behind in her old house, and she was a new Amelia now, one who spent the day thinking about where she and Horatio would go next and didn't feel guilty about it at all.

In fact she didn't even remember about the surprise until they were on the way home, but all Mrs. Howling would do when Amelia asked was smile mysteriously.

Fine. Amelia had a secret too. A better secret.

Nonetheless she couldn't concentrate on her homework, and she'd been in her room for hours and Horatio hadn't appeared. She tried calling him, though he hadn't told her when this weekend they'd be going through the twenty-fourth door, and it was only Friday afternoon. The autumn wind whispered through the leaves on the three hundred sixty-five trees outside, their edges turned with the reddish gold of a bonfire. The sun was setting earlier now, and it was low in the sky when Mrs. Howling stood at the bottom of the stairs and called for Amelia.

She dropped her book and ran from her room; it must be time for her to find out whatever her parents were keeping from her. "Yes?" she said excitedly, jumping the last few stairs and landing at the bottom with a thump.

"Careful," her mother chided her. "Could you set the table for me, please?"

Amelia's anticipation turned to annoyance. "Why can't Owen or Matthew do it? They're right there," she said, pointing into the living room. Why did Mum have to call her all the way down from upstairs? Oh, right, because her cousins had been through *so much* already.

"I'm almost at the end of my level," called Owen.

"And I'm watching my show," said Matthew.

"Please, Amie, come and do it," said Mrs. Howling. Grumbling, Amelia followed her mother into the kitchen and waited as Mrs. Howling got cutlery from a drawer.

"If this is my surprise," said Amelia, "it's rubbish."

Mrs. Howling laughed. "It's not. Here you go."

One by one, Amelia put the knives and forks down in their places, circling the long table. When Mum had her back turned, stirring something on the stove, Amelia licked Owen's fork, just for fun.

"Mum, you gave me too many." Amelia held up the extra silverware. Lavender was much too young to use real ones; she had special plastic ones that she mostly used to hammer loudly on the table. Any food Lavender actually managed to get into her mouth was purely accidental.

"Did I? Oh," said her mother, back still turned. "Why don't you put them next to your place for now."

Puzzle pieces clicked together in Amelia's brain. "Who's coming to dinner?" she asked. For the briefest moment she imagined it might be Horatio, sitting there as he had at the supper outside of time, gesturing with his arm in its dusty sleeve. But of course it wouldn't be him. Only she knew about him.

"I think you're about to find out," said Mum, cocking her head to one side. "Your father's back."

Amelia dropped the last knife and fork on the table with a clatter, ran to the front door, and threw it open. Sure enough, there was Dad's car, with an extra shadow in it in the gathering darkness. A pair of dirty sneakers emerged as the door opened, then a very familiar red head, and Amelia felt her smile grow as wide as the door frame in which she stood.

Izzy.

"We would've been here earlier, but Mum and Dad said I had to go to school today," said Isabelle, sitting beside Amelia at the table. She looked as if she thoroughly disagreed with her parents' decision, but shrugged. "Then your dad came and picked me up right after and we drove all the way here. Mum and Dad said they'll fetch me on Sunday, so we have two whole nights!"

"We thought you girls might like to see each other," said Mr. Howling. He looked tired from spending all day in the car, but he smiled gently at Amelia.

Amelia grinned back. "Come on, Izzy," she said. "I want to show you my room." She jumped up, looked at her parents as an afterthought. "May we be excused?"

"Of course, girls," said Mrs. Howling. "Come down in a little while; there's an apple crumble in the oven, and I got ice cream to have with it."

Izzy *and* crumble. This had turned into a very good day. "Don't eat it all," she said to Owen and Matthew, putting on her best stern face.

"You'd better hurry up, then," said Owen. Amelia stuck her tongue out at him and remembered she'd licked the fork in his hand. Ha.

Isabelle followed Amelia from the kitchen and stopped in the entrance hall. "This house is enormous," she said. "Do you ever get lost in it?"

"A little bit, at first," said Amelia. They clomped up the stairs and into her room, past the letters on her door. She kept meaning to ask Mum if she could take them down, but somehow she always forgot.

"This is nice," said Isabelle. She stood in the middle of the room and turned in a circle, taking in the window seat and the fireplace and all of Amelia's new furniture.

Amelia jumped on her bed and sat cross-legged, patting the space beside her. "It's okay," she said, "but tell me everything about home."

There was quite a lot for Izzy to tell, it seemed. Amelia listened to everything that had happened to their old friends since she'd moved away, and about all the new friends Izzy had made, even though she'd mentioned most of this in her letter. Her *one* letter. Amelia had only written once in all the time they'd been apart too, but she had good reasons, like the house and Horatio and their adventures. There *was* news for Izzy to share: Mrs. Frenkel was having a baby, and soon she'd be leaving the school for a little while to look after it. Izzy didn't know who the new librarian would be, though she hoped it would be somebody nice. The new neighbors were nice too, the ones who'd moved into Amelia's house, but they didn't seem interested in becoming friends with Izzy's parents. Which was fine with Izzy, who didn't want to be running around after a little kid all the time.

Amelia knew the feeling. Not that she ran around after Lavender much, but she babbled all the time, when she wasn't crying, and her crying was the only noise in the world shrill enough to be heard throughout the entire house.

Mrs. Howling knocked and entered with two bowls of crumble and ice cream, rescued from the boys. They thanked her and waited until she'd closed the door again. It was just like it used to be, the two of them tucked away in Amelia's room, or Izzy's, ready for a sleepover. They'd stay up far later than they were supposed to, whisper-giggling under the covers until they couldn't keep their eyes open anymore. Amelia's parents and Izzy's parents had long ago given up putting a spare bed in the room on such nights; in the morning the girls were always found together, because it was easier to talk really quietly in the same bed.

"So, what's it like living here with your cousins?" Isabelle asked, and it all came back to Amelia with a rush. How much she'd hated it to begin with, how alone she'd felt even in a more crowded house than she ever had before. How scared—and intrigued— she'd been when she first started to think the house was haunted.

And how she'd been right, in a way.

Horatio. She'd almost forgotten about Horatio since Izzy had arrived. But how much could she tell her? Amelia looked at her friend and remembered all the secrets she'd ever told Izzy that Izzy had never repeated to anyone. Everything. She could tell Izzy everything.

"Well," she began.

The shutters outside her window came loose from their fastenings and slammed closed, rattling the glass. Izzy jumped. *It was just the wind*, Amelia told herself.

The wind could get strong here, what was a slight breeze in the town gathering speed over the treetops as it rushed to Nudiustertian House.

"It's . . ."

The light in its fixture overhead flickered. Amelia swallowed. An old house, with wonky heating and wonky wires.

"There's—"

Silence, Amelia, said the house's voice inside her head. Horatio's voice. *Hold your tongue.*

Fear tingled up Amelia's spine. He'd never sounded so angry with her before. She took a deep breath. "There's good things about it," she said. "It's not so bad."

The shutters banged open.

There was a foot in Amelia's face. At some point in the night Isabelle had completely flipped around in bed, and she must have been too warm, too, because she was atop the covers, snoring. Amelia turned her head, saw the shape on the wall. It raised a hand, curled its fingers like someone making shadow puppets, beckoning her.

She climbed from the bed, pausing, breath held, as Izzy turned over. Another snore filled the room, and

Amelia left it, following Horatio across the landing, up the stairs to the attic. As many times as she'd seen him turn into a man, it never stopped being a little bit weird. The early-morning sunlight streaming through the oddly shaped window was weak and thin, but it caught his amber ring, made it sparkle and glow.

"Amelia," he began. He did not sound as furious as he had the night before when he'd spoken inside her head, but there remained an edge of something in his voice.

"I know what you're going to say, and Izzy wouldn't tell anyone." Amelia glared at him, arms folded over her chest. He wasn't the only one who could get angry.

"I am not concerned by that, so much," said Horatio. "Who would believe her? Who, besides her, would believe you? No, Amelia, that is not my worry. My worry is that I have made a mistake."

"What mistake?" Amelia said. Her voice shook, and she didn't want it to.

Horatio paced the bare wooden floor, skirting around the boxes of photographs Amelia had moved up here. "A mistake in choosing you," he said. "I thought you would be strong enough to do what we do. I thought you would want the life that we have."

"I do!" said Amelia. She wanted to travel time

forever, to build her own calendar house and be magic like Horatio and Madame Roseline and Felix and all the others.

"Are you certain?" he asked, cocking his head.

"Yes!"

"You need to be certain, Amelia. You need to understand that when the time comes, you will leave all of this behind. You will no longer have human friends in whom you can confide your secrets, at least not for a long time. Perhaps, one day, you will do what I have done and find an apprentice, but until then you will only have the others of your kind for company. They will become your friends, your family, because they are there and they will understand. They won't be people you choose."

"Is that why you wanted an apprentice? So you could choose someone? Have a family?"

"It is the only way I can," said Horatio, staring out the window. "But I fear I have chosen someone who is too attached to her world and her time, who won't be able to give it all up in order to gain the whole world and all of time. I have seen what happens to those of us who cannot let go, who find our life unpleasant. It is not a thing I'd wish upon anyone. Nor do I understand it, for this is the greatest existence there is."

"Who?" demanded Amelia. "Who doesn't like it? Have I met them?"

"That is not my story to tell; I doubt you will ever hear it. My point is, my dear, you need to be willing to let everyone forget you."

Amelia swallowed. "I am," she said, too loudly.

"Who are you talking to?" Izzy asked, stomping up the stairs. In an eyeblink Horatio was a shadow again, and then he was gone.

"Nobody."

"I could've sworn I heard you talking."

"Not me," said Amelia, forcing a smile onto her face. She'd never lied to Izzy before, not once. "Maybe you're still dreaming."

"D'you know, I can't remember what I dreamed. Oh, well. Breakfast! I can hear your Mum downstairs."

Amelia trailed Izzy all the way down to the kitchen, her mind whirring. So Horatio didn't believe she was good enough, and if she wasn't good enough, he'd stop taking her on adventures. He'd disappear back into the shadows for good, and she'd be left alone, even more alone than she was before he showed himself, because she'd know he was there, ignoring her.

They'd been planning another adventure this weekend, before Izzy arrived. And she could still go, with

Izzy here, time pausing in the house while Amelia and
Horatio went somewhere wonderful, but she was posi-
tive he wouldn't take her now, not until he was sure
she'd meant what she'd said in the attic.

She would have to prove it to him. Prove she was
willing to forget all about Mum and Dad and Izzy and
everyone to become his family instead.

Deep in thought, Amelia took her place at the table.
For once, Mum had made plenty of pancakes, a giant
stack of them dripping with butter. Lavender thumped
her spoon and plastic cup happily on the table. Amelia
ate in near silence, mumbling thanks when Matthew
passed her the bottle of syrup.

"I want to go outside," Isabelle declared when she
was finished. "We drove through all those trees when I
came, but it was too dark to really see anything."

A sick feeling swirled in Amelia's stomach, oozing
like the melting butter. She knew all too well that once
Isabelle had made up her mind about something, it
was almost impossible to change. "I don't," said Amelia.
Izzy blinked at her.

"What's got you in a grump?"

"Nothing," Amelia snapped.

"Girls—" said Mr. Howling.

"Fine. Maybe Owen wants to come outside."

Owen shrugged. "Sure. Matthew can come, too. We'll show you where we found the frog one time." Amelia bit her lip. How dare he be so happy to steal her friend! He had friends of his own; he didn't need hers. But she couldn't leave Izzy with no one to play with or show her the forest.

"*Excellent.* Frogs are awesome. Come on!"

The front door slammed a moment later, joining in with Lavender's gleeful banging. "What was that about?" Mrs. Howling asked Amelia. "Did you two quarrel in the night?"

"No," said Amelia. "I just don't feel like playing outside today."

"Isabelle came all this way to see you, Amie, and your dad drove all day to fetch her. Sometimes we have to do things we don't want."

"I know." She did know. She wanted to be outside with Izzy and the others, running around, looking for frogs if that's what Izzy felt like doing, but instead she was in the kitchen with Mum and Dad giving her strange, worried looks.

"You know how it goes, Susan," said her father to her mother. "At their age I went from best friends to enemies to best friends again in five minutes. Give them a bit of time; they'll sort it out."

"You're right," said Mrs. Howling. "Okay, sweetheart, if you're not going outside, you're going to help me with the washing up."

"Fine," said Amelia. Mum fetched her a stool and she stood at the sink, scrubbing syrup from the plates as she looked out the window into the garden. Izzy and Owen were doing handstands in the grass; Matthew was trying but kept falling over. Through the glass Amelia heard Izzy's laughter when Matthew stood up for the third time, his face covered in dirt. A tear dripped from her chin and plopped into the soapy water. Her mother dried and put away the last dish and Amelia stepped down from the stool, kept walking all the way to the library. From here she couldn't hear them playing without her.

"See?" she said, not knowing if Horatio was bothering to listen. Perhaps he had completely given up on her. "I can do it."

"I see," he said, emerging from the shadows. "And you will tell your parents you don't want her visiting again?"

Another tear beaded at the corner of Amelia's eye. "Yes," she said, "but can I go play with her, just for now? I promise when the time comes I'll say goodbye." Suddenly she didn't understand how Owen or

Matthew ever smiled or laughed at all. Sure, they were still sad a lot of the time, but they were happy sometimes too. And they hadn't *known* they were saying good-bye to Uncle Hugo and Aunt Marie until after it happened. They'd had no warning.

Horatio nodded. "Yes. Once she has gone, we shall go on our next adventure. Well done, Amelia."

CHAPTER ELEVEN

Pirates

H E HADN'T ASKED HER WHERE she wanted to go, which was a good thing. Amelia had a vivid imagination—the adventures she had with Isabelle were proof of that—and she couldn't have thought of this. Well, she could have, but not as quickly as Horatio did, leading her to the twenty-fourth door and opening it onto the most incredible thing she'd ever seen. Reading about these things wasn't the same; when she was curled up with a book, she had to pretend she could hear the ocean or wrinkle her nose just at the thought of the barrels of fish lining the docks. Now she was close enough to touch their glassy, slimy eyes if she wished.

She kept her hands to herself, and her thoughts. There would be no more adventures with Isabelle, would there?

People crushed around them, dressed in salt-crusted rags, and there was shouting, so much shouting. Again Amelia didn't understand what they were saying, but that was less surprising here. They were not only in a different time, but clearly a very different place, too. Never had the difference been so marked. The first time Horatio had taken her anywhere, it had been winter, and every other time the people they'd seen had been in suits, long gowns, armor. Here, people's arms and legs were bare, their clothing thin, and they were trying to cool themselves with huge, folding fans, or their hands if they didn't have those. What skin she could see on faces and arms was shiny with sweat. Clearly it was as hot as on the holiday she'd taken with Mum and Dad in the desert, perhaps hotter.

Amelia shivered in her jumper.

"Do you know what they're saying?" she asked. "My mum speaks a lot of languages; it's what she does for a job."

"But of course. I've had ample opportunity in which to learn every language ever spoken, and some that haven't been invented yet in your time. I can see the question on your face, Amelia. I bring you to the past more than I take you to the future because where we come from is often more interesting than where we are going. Look, for example, at that."

An enormous ship rose from the water, a black flag strung from its tallest mast. A gust of wind blew as she craned her neck; the flag billowed, and the sunlight shone off the white skull and crossbones.

"I thought that was a thing they made up for stories."

Horatio twitched, annoyed, as if one of the hundreds of stinging, buzzing bugs floating on the humid air had flown into his ear with her words.

"We have company today," he said, pointing through a gap between two people. Madame Roseline and Felix waited at the water's edge, Madame Roseline's pale face shadowed by a dainty lace parasol. She did not look to be dressed particularly warmly; perhaps she was used to the cold after all this time. "Good morning, dear friends."

"Horatio, and Amelia! It is lovely to see you both," said Madame Roseline. "Felix, say hello."

"Horatio," said Felix, bowing. "Amelia, are you well?"

His stiff politeness made Amelia laugh. "Yes, thank

you," she said, in the poshest voice she could muster. She'd never been very good at doing the voices. Dad was; when he read her bedtime stories, he *always* did the voices, each one sounding different from the last, but her father hadn't read her a bedtime story since they'd moved to Nudiustertian House. For an instant it felt as if a cloud had passed over the sun, and then came the first warm thing she'd felt, brought by Madame Roseline taking her hand.

"Thank you for helping," Horatio said to her. Amelia's eyebrows creased, and she looked up at Madame Roseline, who waved Horatio's thanks off with a gesture of her elegant hand.

"Anything for you, and this charming young girl, who will be joining our number soon enough. Isn't that right, Amelia? Has Horatio been showing you all the wonderful things you can see and do if you become one of us?"

"In fact, we were just discussing that," said Horatio. "I believe I have mentioned that Amelia here is a great lover of books, of words. Imagine, Amelia, if you could understand every word ever spoken, read every book in every language. Know even more than your mother. And you would have the time to do so."

Amelia closed her eyes, felt the sun turn her eyelids

orange-pink. The library at the house was full of books, more than she'd be able to read in a normal lifetime.

Horatio was offering her far more than a normal lifetime. "That sounds brilliant," she said.

"Excellent. Now, let us have a grand old time. Horatio, are we staying on land, or shall we take to the high seas?"

Horatio winked. "I believe that's up to Amelia."

Amelia turned back and forth, looking from the island to the water. Fear flickered in her belly, down to her toes. Playing at the seaside was all right, but she'd never told anyone how frightened she was of the ocean. Wide, deep, black waters with *anything* lurking beneath the surface. Mum and Dad had wanted to go on a trip on a boat once, but Amelia had begged them to visit the top of a mountain instead. Sharks and giant squids couldn't get her at the top of a mountain.

Felix leaned down, an odd smile on his face. "You can't get hurt while you're with us," he whispered, too quiet for Horatio or Madame Roseline to hear him. "I was afraid of it too."

"You promise?"

"Promise."

"The boat," said Amelia. Despite Felix's assurance, she clung tight to Madame Roseline as they slipped through the crowd of people who didn't know they were there, along the busy dock, and onto the deck of a ship whose captain had no idea he suddenly had four extra passengers. Horatio led the way to the prow, but Amelia stopped, staring at a man who had a hook where his hand should be. Another thing she'd thought they made up for stories.

There was a word for what they were. *Stowaways.* At home time was frozen, frozen at the moment when Matthew was playing a computer game and Owen was doing multiplication homework and Lavender was covering things with sticky fingerprints. Her father had been sweeping the first fallen leaves from the driveway, her mother sorting through a pile of papers. Normal, ordinary, *boring* things.

And Amelia was stowed away on a pirate ship. She clapped, her lingering fear of the water forgotten, and ran over the wet, slippery deck to join the others. Horatio twirled and leaped up onto the railing, teetering over the water. Amelia gasped, peeked through her fingers as he danced along. Surely he was going to fall, but of course he did not, and soon she was giggling at his elaborate steps. Even Madame Roseline allowed herself a delicate laugh. Finally he jumped back to the deck, and Amelia moved toward him, skidding on the treacherous wood. Felix caught her, swung her up, and sat her on the very edge of the railing, her feet—in shoes, which she wore all the time now, unless she was in bed, just in case—dangling over the depths. Behind her Horatio and Madame Roseline were now discussing plans for their next dinner party. Would Horatio take her with him?

"Do remember it is your turn to bring dessert, Horatio."

"Yes, I know. Perhaps this is not the right time to discuss it, however." His voice sounded strange, but Felix had such a tight grip on her shoulders Amelia couldn't twist enough to see Horatio's face, so she looked at Felix's hands instead. They were bare, the fingernails chewed and ragged. He did not wear an amber ring.

"We're moving," said Felix. The lace at his cuffs tickled Amelia's chin, and she turned her face back to the ocean. There was nothing to see, no land except that behind them, but everything was out there. Amid shouts that were clearly commands in the foreign language, and the snapping of sails in the wind, and running footsteps, one voice boomed. It came closer. The hook caught the railing right beside Amelia. The grinning, toothless face of the man it belonged to stared right through her as he waved his other hand in the air. The hook was cleaner. Amelia held tight; the ship gathered speed. She trusted Felix, and he wasn't letting her fall, but it was still all so difficult to believe.

It was like being in a book. All of it had been, except the first time, when Horatio had taken her to her own house, or what had been her house, in the future. Old London, a castle and a joust, a pirate ship leaving an island halfway across the world. Places and things she'd read about, never for a moment thinking she would get to see them with her own eyes.

She could see them forever, and when she ran out of places she could think of, she'd read about more. She wouldn't look old, like Horatio, or possibly as young as Felix, though she wasn't certain about that. Horatio hadn't told her exactly how long it would take to make her one of them. Maybe she would end up like Madame Roseline, once everyone who had remembered her had died: Mum and Dad, Owen and Matthew and Lavender. It was a sad thought; she didn't want any of them to die, but it wouldn't happen soon, and that made it all right, didn't it? Yes. She would be as elegant and well-spoken as Madame Roseline, traveling through time from her own calendar house. It would have turrets and hidden staircases, fireplaces, and a library better even than the one at Nudiustertian House, which she could still only pronounce in her head, where there was no one to tell her she'd gotten it wrong.

She'd give her house a better name, and nice people would live in it while she went on adventures just like this one.

Across the vast ocean a shadow shimmered on the horizon. Not a shadow like Horatio, but actually, it was a bit like that. A shadow at first, but as the ship sped toward it, it became something else. Another ship, maybe even larger than the one on which Amelia sat on the railing. Ropes whistled, and shouts from the crew swelled behind her like the rising waves below her dangling feet. They weren't slowing down; they were speeding up. If they didn't stop soon, they were going to run right into the other ship.

Amelia remembered where she was, the books she'd read. A pirate ship.

"Oh!" said Madame Roseline. "Excitement. Amelia, will you be frightened?"

"No," said Amelia, not entirely sure if that was true, but still sure that if Horatio or Madame Roseline, or even Felix, thought she was too much of a scaredy-cat to handle their adventures, they wouldn't make her one of them.

"Good girl—however, Felix? Perhaps lift her down; there's a dear." Just as Madame Roseline spoke, the ship pitched to one side, Amelia's stomach tilting along with it. Felix set her down easily on the deck, holding her shoulders until he was certain Amelia was steady on her feet. She didn't protest.

Besides, now she could see everything happening on the deck. The pirates were running everywhere, barking orders in gravelly voices, sliding stones along blades that already looked sharp enough to slice the very air in two. Their clothes were filthy rags, ill-fitting and badly stitched, but they kept their knives like new. Amelia understood that. Her room could be messy, her jeans muddy, but she never let anything happen to her books.

Four of the men heaved and pushed something enormous across the spray-slicked wood, its rusted wheels creaking. A cannon.

"They won't use it unless they have to," said Horatio. "They don't want to damage their quarry."

"They want the boat," said Amelia. "Right?"

"Yes," Felix agreed. "And anything on it, but the boat itself would be prize enough. Take a proper look around, Amelia."

She thought she had when they'd first stepped on

board; it wasn't fair that Felix assumed she hadn't just because she was young . . . or just because she was human. Even as she prepared to argue, though, she squinted, saw the signs of wear on the deck, the frayed ropes, the bedraggled sails. They were close enough now to really see the other ship, new and whole, all its woodwork shining in the sun. It was much nicer, much larger, a better home on which to live on the seas.

But that was something else that wasn't fair. "It's their boat," she said. "Taking it just because the pirates want it isn't . . . It isn't *right*, is it?"

Madame Roseline's eyes darted to Horatio, who swallowed deeply. He kneeled down so his face was level with Amelia's. "Sometimes, Amelia, it is necessary to take the thing you need in order to stay alive, or to fulfill who you are. You have read books about pirates, yes? What about books about animals, like lions or tigers?"

"Of course," answered Amelia, who didn't see what that had to do with anything.

"Then you know that lions or tigers have to hunt other animals for food. They chase down the antelope. Even humans do this. For a lion to do otherwise would make it . . . not a lion. It is part of its very nature. So too with these pirates. This is the life they know, likely the only life they have ever known. Many of them will have been raised on rum and mayhem from the time they were infants. It is not in a pirate's nature to see a thing he does not have, a thing he may need or want, and not attempt to take it for himself. Oh, sometimes the attempt will fail, but that will only make him smarter, wiser the next time. This ship we stand on would have been obtained the same way, and the one before that. Like a hermit crab, moving to a bigger shell each time it grows, this crew, ably led by their captain, must move into a larger, better ship in order to survive. It is who they are, Amelia. It is what they *must do*, and therefore it is right."

Horatio's dark eyes were sparkling once more; he didn't look tired at all today, like he had when they were at the castle and the joust. Amelia looked to Madame Roseline, who nodded in eager agreement with Horatio's words, and Felix, who smiled and turned quickly away to watch the men load the cannon.

"How does it end?" she asked. "Do they get it? Have you been here before?"

"Watch and see."

The water played tricks on her eyes. The other ship seemed close enough to touch now, though she knew if she reached out, she would topple into the waves, sink down to the sharks and giant squids and whatever else flicked its fins or gnashed its giant teeth in anticipation. They were close enough for the captain, a few yards from Amelia, to raise an odd kind of horn to his lips and speak through it, his counterpart on the other ship shaking both his head and his fist in response. Everywhere, on both decks, the men were preparing to fight, one crew to take, the other to defend.

A man at the top of a mast high over Amelia's head threw down a rope that whistled past her ear. Another man caught it and ran, sure-footed on the slippery deck. He leaped over the railing and flew over the depths, swinging on the rope as she'd done from tree branches once in an adventure park. All at once a dozen others joined him, jumping from the ship and letting go of the ropes when they were at their highest, dropping down, their blades out before they'd landed on their feet on the other ship. Amelia blinked, the captain shouted, Madame Roseline clapped her hands in glee. Something—and Amelia knew exactly what, but couldn't bring herself to think it—toppled down the side and landed with a sickening splash.

This was different from the joust; that had just been a game. The knight had hopped up from the dirt and bowed crookedly to the king. There were no kings here.

Under the harsh sunlight the entire thing took both hours and no time at all. Knives clashed; the captain of the larger ship fell to his knees; the captain of this one raised his horn to his mouth again. Horatio explained that he was giving the other man a choice: surrender and become part of the crew, or face certain death. Amelia knew which one she'd choose, and it seemed the man agreed with her, raising his arms in defeat this time, not defiance.

So, they'd let him live. Maybe that made the whole thing all right. Yes, the pirates were still taking something that didn't belong to them, but together with the other crew they'd live on the larger ship until *it* wasn't big enough, at which point they'd do the same thing again. It was who they were, who all of them were.

Amelia's feet skidded as the two ships bumped against each other, and with Horatio and Madame Roseline and Felix she watched the crew begin to move all their possessions over to the other one. She wondered if any of the men felt like she had the day she'd moved to Nudiustertian House, already homesick for her old one. Probably pirates didn't think like that. Probably none of them had grown up on this exact ship, and therefore weren't sad to leave it. Still, she saw a few of them carrying sacks and crates more gently than their strong arms and grizzled faces should allow, just as she'd insisted that her prized dictionary travel with her in the car so nothing happened to it.

People everywhere, everywhen, were the same.

Horatio checked his funny pocket watch and nodded to Madame Roseline. Clearly it was time to leave, though Horatio *had* kept his promise. They'd stayed out for hours, and it was occurring to Amelia that it had been an awfully long time since breakfast. She didn't know if she was actually hungry, if enough time had passed for her to be hungry, or if that was just what her mind was telling her. Either way, she wouldn't say no to a sandwich if Mum was in the mood to make one when she got home. Not that Mum would know Amelia had gone anywhere. She'd kept her word too, and she hadn't been afraid, but perhaps next time she'd ask for a slightly quieter adventure.

CHAPTER TWELVE

Troublesome Truths

THE BELL RANG, SIGNALING THE end of lunch. Amelia trudged behind Owen, back to Mrs. Murdoch's classroom. They'd done math and science already this morning; now it was time for English and history. Amelia took her usual seat in the back, tucking her bag underneath her desk. It was heavier than usual, full of books about times and places she wanted to ask Horatio if they could go. Some of the stories in the books were as exciting as any of the made-up ones she'd read, which Amelia supposed made sense, when she thought about it. She was thinking about a lot of things now that had never occurred to her before, and one of them was definitely that people took exciting things that had really happened and mixed them into other things they'd imagined, like pirates and children who could fly, or kings and castles and magic. People who wrote books borrowed the world's memories and made them even better.

Mrs. Murdoch was passing out sheets of paper; Amelia had to wait until the very last to see what was on hers. It was a list of words the students needed to define, and that would have been interesting if Amelia didn't know all of them already. Owen might be faster than her at multiplication, but this was easy. She pulled a newly sharpened pencil—for there hadn't been much else to do at lunchtime—from her bag and quickly wrote down all the answers.

Excellent. Now she could go back to thinking about the pirates, and the house. Not Nudiustertian House, but her own. Right before he'd disappeared after the adventure with the pirates, after Madame Roseline and Felix had bid their old-fashioned farewells, Horatio had given her homework. At first she'd thought he was going to ask her to write a report on what she'd seen, but instead he'd told her it was time to begin think-ing about what she'd want her own calendar house to be like. She hadn't told him that she'd already started thinking about it, because then when she gave him all her ideas, it would look as if she'd done it all so quickly, and he would again marvel at how clever she was.

Along with the heavy books, in Amelia's overstuffed bag was a stack of magazines she'd asked Mum if she could have. She'd had to promise to be careful with the scissors she'd needed too, in case she came across a picture of a house that was anything like the one in her head.

There wouldn't be one that was exactly like it, anywhere. Only in Amelia's head did her great, grand, beautiful house exist. Horatio had warned her not to get too impatient yet, that it would take a long time—years, perhaps—to design it, and it had to be perfect. Once they started to build it, they couldn't make the smallest mistake, because if there was an extra stair or one window fewer than there was supposed to be, the house wouldn't work. Still, in her mind Amelia walked from room to room, knowing precisely how the sunlight would fall on the floor, or the echo rain would make when it hammered the windows. A library full of books would—

"Ahem."

The imagined house vanished, replaced by the all-too-real face of Mrs. Murdoch, standing over Amelia. Her arms were folded over her chest, lips thinned into a straight line.

"Yes, Mrs. Murdoch?"

"You are to work in my class, Amelia, not daydream."

"But I'm finished," said Amelia, turning over her paper so Mrs. Murdoch could see her answers, all filled in. Mrs. Murdoch's lips thinned to complete invisibility and she plucked the paper from Amelia's desk with sharp, yellowed fingernails. Her eyes darted back and forth as she read, and Amelia wondered if she'd gotten the answers wrong, but then Mrs. Murdoch's shoulders suddenly relaxed.

"Well done, Amelia," she said. It was the first time in the month Amelia had been in her class that Mrs. Murdoch had smiled at her. "I'm sorry; I jumped to conclusions when I saw you staring out the window." She lowered her voice to a whisper. "I have some more difficult ones in my desk; would you like to try one of those?"

Well, yes and no. Amelia wanted to think about her house some more, but it was probably a good idea to keep this teacher happy too. "All right," said Amelia, nodding. "Thank you."

Owen's eyes were on Amelia as Mrs. Murdoch fetched the promised paper and set it on Amelia's desk with another smile. She looked up and caught him glaring, like Mrs. Murdoch was his teacher, and Amelia wasn't allowed to get along with her. Like Amelia should have pretended not to know the answers.

Amelia stuck her tongue out at him. Mrs. Murdoch had her back to both of them, and Mrs. Howling wasn't here to tell Amelia she'd freeze that way. Owen's eyes narrowed for an instant before he turned them back to his own paper, the first one he'd been given, because he wasn't as good at words as Amelia. So there.

She had just written the last definition on her special worksheet when Mrs. Murdoch cleared her throat. It was time for them all to put away their English work and take out their history books. Back home, Amelia and Isabelle had always agreed that history wasn't as much fun as English, but Amelia wasn't sure she still believed that. Now that she could visit anywhere in time the same way she could visit the words in her enormous dictionary, it was all more exciting. Amelia rested her elbows on her desk and waited for instructions, eager now to prove to Mrs. Murdoch that she could be as good at other things as she was at definitions.

"Today, class, we are going to begin to look at medieval times," said Mrs. Murdoch, writing the words down on the chalkboard as she spoke. "Does anyone know what I mean?"

"You mean when there were kings," said a girl across the room, twirling a red curl around her finger and sounding bored. Even the back of her head looked bored.

"Very good, Jessica," said Mrs. Murdoch, "but we still have kings, and queens. What else?" She added *royalty* to the chalkboard.

"Castles," said Owen.

"Kings and queens have to live somewhere, but we still have those, too."

Amelia wriggled in her seat, raising her hand like Jessica and Owen should have done. Mrs. Murdoch faced the class and pointed at her. "Yes, Amelia?"

"There were jousts and other games and . . ." Amelia closed her eyes, talking as she remembered everything she'd seen with Horatio. The way the knights had bowed, and the divots in the ground when the horses stamped and reared, colored silks rippling from their flanks. She described the queen, her crown glinting, and the dented armor. And then, then there were the more ordinary parts of castle life from after they'd left the games: cows being milked and buzzing hives of bees, bread being baked in enormous ovens. The thrones had been plain wood, not gold as Amelia had imagined before seeing them, covered with embroidered cushions. She'd climbed a winding stone staircase, peered through a strange, tall, thin window with no glass in it, which Horatio had said was for shooting arrows through if anyone tried to attack the castle.

"And that's . . . that's the way it was," Amelia finished, suddenly painfully aware of the hush that had fallen on the classroom, and every student twisted at their desks to gape at her.

"That was . . . that was very detailed, Amelia," said Mrs. Murdoch. "Good for you. Did you read about this in a book?"

Owen laughed. "Probably," he said, punching his friend next to him lightly on the shoulder. "She *always* has her face in a book. Thinks she's better than the rest of us, that nothing is as good as her precious books."

Anger seethed inside Amelia. So what if she did? But anyway, she didn't anymore. She was having adventures with Horatio, which was more than Owen could say. "No," she said, scowling at him. "I've seen it."

The entire class burst out laughing. Mrs. Murdoch herself allowed a small twitch to flutter her lips before she got control of it. "Sometimes reading about something *does* feel like seeing it—right, Amelia?"

She knew she wasn't supposed to tell, but Owen was still laughing at her, even after Mrs. Murdoch gestured for everyone to shush. He picked up his textbook and shoved his face as far into it as it would go, nose wedged right in the middle.

"I've *seen* it," Amelia insisted. "And pirate ships and Queen Victoria having her picture taken and—"

"Enough!" said Mrs. Murdoch, both to Amelia and to the renewed laughter around her. "Everyone, please settle down. Amelia, please gather your things and follow me."

A hot, dark, heavy thing fell with a thud into Amelia's stomach. She was in trouble. She'd never been in trouble at school, and now she was, just for telling the truth. Owen snickered quietly as she yanked her bag from under her desk and stomped to the door, tears prickling her eyes.

Voices came from behind a closed door. Amelia couldn't make out the words. Maybe when Mrs. Murdoch had taken her into the corridor and asked her why she was telling fibs, Amelia should've agreed that she was. She could've just said that making up stories was fun—she and Isabelle used to do it, though never in class—and she'd gotten carried away. If she'd apologized, maybe Mrs. Murdoch wouldn't have called her mother.

The door opened a crack. "I will speak to her," said

Mrs. Howling to the others behind the door. "I'm sure we can all agree that it is simply a case of Amelia having some difficulty adjusting to her new life here. She has always done well in school."

"She is clearly extraordinarily bright," said Mrs. Murdoch's voice. "A pleasure to have in class when she's not disrupting it. Thank you for coming in."

The door opened wider, and Mrs. Howling stepped out, Lavender on her hip and a harried expression on her face. "Come, darling, we'll discuss this at home," she said, holding out her free hand to tug Amelia from her chair. "Let's wait for Owen and Matthew in the car."

It probably wasn't a good time to suggest not waiting for them at all, so Amelia only pretended to say it. Mrs. Howling strapped Lavender back into her special car seat and climbed in behind the wheel, leaning back against the headrest as Amelia buckled her seat belt. Now that she'd had time to calm down, she realized it would be a very bad idea to insist to her mother that she had been telling the truth about everything she'd seen, and if they discussed it back at the house, Horatio could be listening in. He'd find out that Amelia couldn't be trusted to keep a secret, and then he might change his mind altogether about teaching her to be a time-traveling shadow-person with her own calendar house.

"I'm sorry, Mum," said Amelia in a small voice. "I just got mad."

"I know," said Mrs. Howling. "Oh, sweetheart. Sometimes when you don't want to be where you are, it's nicer to imagine being somewhere else, isn't it? Like a castle or a pirate ship? I know you're homesick, and I know you're still angry with me and Dad for selling the house, but you are going to have to understand that we are staying here."

"I know we are," said Amelia. "I don't want to leave."

"Oh," said Mum, surprised. She looked at Amelia, in the front seat beside her, over the top of the glasses she wore for driving. "Well, that's a good start. We're all going to have a family discussion at dinner about how to keep making this easier, all right?"

"All right." Now that she knew no time passed for everyone else while she was off with Horatio, Amelia could afford to be a little more generous with family time, if that was what Mum insisted on. She didn't need to be so careful about hiding herself away where no one would come looking for her.

That did, however, mean spending time with them, and *them* included Owen. Blech. His mocking laughter still rang in her ears. The car door opened, and there was his stupid face, followed by Matthew's slightly less stupid face. Matthew hadn't done anything to annoy her today.

"Hi, Aunt Susan," said Matthew, whacking Amelia's shoulder with his bag. Okay, now his face was stupid too.

"Hi, Matthew," said Mrs. Howling. "How was your day?"

"It was okay. Owen said Amelia got in trouble."

Mrs. Howling sighed and glanced at Owen through the little mirror hanging over the windshield. "Owen, just because Amelia got in trouble, that doesn't mean you aren't in trouble too, but we will talk about this after supper."

They rode back to Nudiustertian House in silence, Owen's a very sulking silence. Amelia fled from the car as soon as it had come to a stop, running up the stairs to her bedroom. Horatio hadn't said he'd come for her today, but she wanted to have as much of her house done as possible in case he did. Cross-legged on her bed, she pored over the magazines Mum had given her, drawing circles around balconies and funny arched doorways with one of the markers she kept in her pencil case.

Supper was silent too, except for Lavender banging her sticky fists beside her plate. Amelia chewed and watched her father, the top of his head shining through his thinning hair under the light from the chandelier over the table. Purple marks smudged under his eyes; he never used to look so tired. He'd been so busy working at the new job he'd had to get when they moved here, or tidying up the garden, which was so much larger than the one at their old house. Mum looked tired as well, now that Amelia looked at her properly over a forkful of mashed potato. She'd gone from having just Amelia to take care of to having Amelia *and* Owen *and* Matthew *and* Lavender, who needed to be stopped from putting sticky handprints on everything all the time. And she worked, too, from the computer in the conservatory.

The hot, sick, heavy thing in Amelia's tummy was back. She'd gotten in trouble for telling the truth, and Owen had laughed at her for it, and now her parents were tired of dealing with everything.

Mrs. Howling set down her glass. "Right," she said. "We need to talk about what happened today."

"Why?" asked Owen sullenly. "Amelia made up stories in class. Punish her."

It was amazing how much Mrs. Howling looked like Mrs. Murdoch when her lips thinned in exactly the same way. "And your teacher said you were making fun of her for liking books, that you laughed at Amelia. Owen, we're family; we don't do that."

"You can't tell me what to do. You're not my mum, and *you're* not my dad."

"That's quite enough," said Mr. Howling. "Your mum and dad wanted us to be in charge if anything ever . . . They wanted us to be in charge. That means they wanted you to listen to us, and for us to look after you. We're doing the very best we can at that, but Owen, you have to be polite, and you have to do as you're told, whichever one of us tells you."

"No, I don't," said Owen. He pushed his plate away. "And I don't have to eat this dinner; I hate it. My mum cooked better."

"What did she cook for you that was so much better?" asked Mrs. Howling.

The cutlery jumped, clanging as Owen smacked his fist on the table. "I can't remember! I can't remember what she cooked! I can't remember what Dad used to say when he dropped us off at school!" Owen's eyes glittered in the light from the chandelier; he wiped them on the back of his hand and pushed his chair back to run from the room. Matthew was a little slower, chasing his brother when he realized no one was going to stop him.

Mr. and Mrs. Howling exchanged a look. "Their

therapist said that was normal," said Amelia's mother. "I mean, I know it is. I can't remember what *my* mum's voice sounded like, though I pretend I can. I hear it in my head, but I have no idea if I'm right."

Amelia's father nodded. "It's a part of grief, of loss, but it's not easy. It can't be easy for them. Or you," he said, taking Mrs. Howling's hand on the table. "He was your brother."

"I need to do a good job with them . . . for him," she said.

All this talk of not remembering, and Amelia herself felt forgotten, sitting there at the table. They were supposed to all be having a discussion on how to be a better family, but instead Owen had shouted and gotten his way; he definitely wasn't going to get in trouble for laughing at her now.

"May I be excused?"

Amelia's father blinked. "Yes. Yes, of course, sweetheart, we're sorry. We'll all have this talk when we're calmer. Do something for me? Save the stories to tell me or Mum?"

"Okay." She nodded. She shouldn't tell those stories to anyone; they'd all think she made them up anyway, the things she'd seen with Horatio and Madame Roseline and Felix.

"Thank you, Amie," said her mother, standing. "I'm going to go find them some more photographs of Hugo and Marie. Maybe that will help."

"I put them in the attic," Amelia reminded her. "The cold downstairs was damaging them."

"That's right." Mum patted her on the head. "Good girl."

Amelia wandered slowly upstairs, counting the railings as she went. She already knew exactly how many there were—she'd counted everything in the house—but it was still good to be sure. She had a house of her own to build soon.

CHAPTER THIRTEEN

First Step, Second Supper

MR. HOWLING WAS STILL IN his jeans, not the suit he usually wore for work. Amelia's heart sank. He wasn't going to fetch Izzy again, was he? But before she could ask, he plucked a whining Lavender from her chair, deposited her on his hip, and looked at Amelia. "I'm going to take you and Matthew to school today, Amie. Are you nearly ready?"

"What about Mum and Owen?" she asked. Owen was still upstairs; she'd thought he was still getting dressed. Mum had given her toast, then gone to the computer in the conservatory.

"Your mother's taking Owen to the doctor."

"Is he sick?" Amelia hadn't heard him sneezing or anything.

"Well, he keeps saying he's forgetting things. We think that's probably normal—I have a memory like a sieve at the best of times—but it's always good to get these things checked out, just to be on the safe side."

"Oh," said Amelia, feeling sorry for him. Spending the day at the doctor instead of school was terrible. And then she remembered how nasty he'd been to her the previous day, and her sympathy vanished with a whoosh. At least he wouldn't be able to do that again. "I just need to put my shoes on."

"Chop-chop," said her father, "and call Matthew down, please."

The ride to school was different without Owen. Quieter. Better, Amelia told herself. She, too, was quiet, not just in the car but all day, choosing not to put her hand up even once. Dad picked them up from school, but Mum and Owen were back when they pulled up the driveway, her car sprinkled with a handful of fallen leaves.

"Did you have a good day, sweetheart?" Mrs. Howling asked, meeting them in the entrance hall.

"It was fine," said Amelia.

"How is he?" asked her father over her head. Mrs. Howling shrugged.

"They said nothing seems wrong, but to keep an eye on it. They'll run more tests if it gets any worse."

"Well, that's good, I suppose."

Amelia ran up the stairs into her room. "Horatio?"

"You're back," he said with a wide smile, stepping out from behind the curtain. "We're going somewhere very special today."

"Where?"

"You'll see. To the twenty-fourth door we go!"

This was a different kind of adventure. First, Horatio took her to see cowboys and old-fashioned trains that coughed steam up to the mountaintops behind the tracks. The dust made Amelia sneeze, so they spent another hour on the shores of Loch Ness at the very moment someone had once claimed to see the monster that supposedly lived in the depths. Unless the monster was a large frog, the person had made it up.

She didn't tell Horatio that *she'd* been accused of making things up. If she had, or if he'd found out another way, he probably wouldn't have brought her here now. Amelia stood on the top of the small hill and looked out at the now, the same now she lived in with Mum and Dad and the others. Horatio could take her to any place, any time, and he'd brought her here for a reason.

"I recall that your previous house was on a hill. I thought perhaps you'd like the same of the next one."

Around the bottom of the hill were fields; church bells rang from a nearby village with red-roofed buildings. In the other direction was a forest that would be green in spring but was now painted with the reds and golds of autumn. For the first time when traveling with Horatio, she was not cold, or not any colder than the weather around her would allow for. Which made sense, as they were only in a different place, not a different time. *Life creates warmth,* Horatio had said, and in this time Amelia was completely human, completely alive.

Though perhaps not for much longer.

"This . . . this is where my house will be?" Amelia asked. It was beautiful. *Perfect* would've been a pond in the swathe of grass that would obviously be the garden; she'd have to put one in like Dad had at her old house.

"It can be wherever you wish. If you don't like this location, we can find another."

"No," said Amelia. "No, it's only that you said it might take years to find the right spot." Without turning her head, Amelia moved her eyes from the treetops to Horatio. He had looked tired again when they were adventuring with the cowboys and the nonexistent monster; now his eyes were sparkling once more. Amelia breathed deeply, the fresh air tinged with smoke like the scent in the attic of Nudiustertian House.

Horatio's old silver-buckled shoes made pointy-toed footprints as he paced. "I thought it might. Certainly, it took me a long time to find the ideal spot. Which I did, of course, just not quickly."

"And was someone helping you, like you're helping me?"

More footprints appeared. Horatio was a dozen feet away now, hands clasped behind his back. "Yes, Amelia, someone helped me. I was found when I was a boy, roughly the same age as you are now, but I did not become what I am until later, because, as I say, it took a long time to find where to build my house."

So the house really was the key. For days she had been cutting out pictures with scissors and drawing in her sketch pad. Only this morning, Mum had accidentally seen what she was doing and had asked Amelia about the turrets. She'd said it looked like a lovely house, and offered Amelia more colored pencils if she needed them. It wasn't such a strange thing for children to draw houses, though; Amelia knew that. There'd been a terrible picture from her very first day of school on the fridge for ages, until she'd begged

Mum to replace it with a spelling test. The spelling test had been there until they'd moved.

Nothing of hers was on the fridge in Nudiustertian House.

"Who was he? Have I met him?"

"You have met *her*," answered Horatio, smiling.

Madame Roseline. Amelia didn't need to ask; she knew she was right. "Was Madame Roseline the first one? Did she have the first calendar house?"

"We believe so," Horatio said. "We do not know. Her memories of her early years are not strong. She could have been made by another, but we have no idea who that would have been. For all we do know, she could have hatched from an egg!"

Amelia laughed, picturing Madame Roseline in her fancy dresses, climbing elegantly from an eggshell. "How did she make the others? You?" For once Horatio was actually answering her. Afternoon sunlight turned the clouds orange, and he tilted his head to the sky, smiling.

"It is a process," he said. "A process that begins at this time, and in this place, should you decide that this is where your calendar house will be, and should you decide again, now that you know what we do, that you wish to become one of us."

The breeze held its breath; the scarlet leaves below stopped rustling. "What will happen to me? Won't my parents notice I'm gone?"

Of course they would, wouldn't they? It couldn't possibly just be like her hiding away in the house, and their only calling for her when it was time for dinner. Mum would notice when she wasn't in the car when it was time for school, and Dad would notice she wasn't in bed when he came to tuck her in. Owen might wonder too, when he wanted someone to laugh at.

The smile on Horatio's face dipped slightly, like the sinking sun behind a cloud. "They will remember," he said, "and then they will forget. Amelia, dear, is that so very different from what is happening already? Once, you were all your mother and father had to think about, and now they are too busy with your cousins to pay attention to you. I have seen it."

A grinding noise filled Amelia's ears; too late she realized it was her teeth. No, it wasn't so very different. Well, they'd be sorry when she left to become something they could never be. She would travel through time; they'd only have one life in which to be boring.

"What do I do?"

A leather satchel sat on the grass, dropped there by Horatio when they'd arrived. He'd been carrying it around all day, if *all day* was the appropriate term when they were outside of time. For once, Amelia wasn't certain of the right word, and for once, it didn't bother her very much. Only a little bit. Her human dictionary didn't have the proper words to describe what Horatio could do—what she would soon be able to do—because it was written by people who hadn't known how to do it. Who hadn't known such things were possible. He opened the flap, and Amelia's fingertips tingled, waiting to see what treasure it held.

Treasure, it turned out, was not the right word.

It was a brick. Heavy in her hand, rough against her palm. Red dust crumbled when she rubbed her thumb across it. Mostly, however, it was just heavy, and it became heavier when Horatio told her where it came from. A brick from the corner of Nudiustertian House, it was the beginning of the magic that would create a new calendar house. When she got back, she was going to find the stone that Madame Roseline had given him. He offered to tell her where it was, but Amelia wanted to find it herself.

"I cannot do it," he said. He wasn't talking about the stone. "You must be the one."

"Why not?"

"Because details have power."

Amelia turned in a circle, looking in all directions from the top of the darkening hill. The village, the woods, the sky. Horatio stepped back as she walked carefully to the very center and set the brick down at her feet. She didn't think that was how you built a house—it would have to be stuck to all the other bricks when she had them—but it was a start.

The start of the magic. There was more to come; she could feel it. The breeze began to blow again, lifting her hair from her neck. Behind her, Horatio was talking about all the finishing touches he'd put on Nudiustertian House, the care he'd taken before letting anyone move into it. The man who wrote the book—it felt like ages since she'd read it—had been right about the three hundred sixty-five trees. For what, asked Horatio, marked the turning of a year better than a tree?

Nothing. Amelia would have a tree. Maybe not a year's worth of them, but one, next to the pond, and from the shadows of the house she'd watch it shake the snow from its branches and wave in the wind. When the house was perfect, every last pane of glass in the windows and the bannisters polished, humans would move in. Humans, because she wouldn't be one anymore, would she? She'd be special, like Horatio, like Madame Roseline, like Felix and all the others.

Her fingertips tingled again. Finally Horatio stopped talking. She should have listened properly—maybe he'd said something important—but when she raised her eyes from the brick, past his silver-buckled shoes and dusty suit, he wore an odd expression. Amelia had felt that expression on her own face before, on her first day of school, before jumping into a lake with Isabelle, before being lifted onto the back of a camel in the desert.

"Do you feel anything?" he asked.

"I think so."

"Good." He inhaled deeply, and his smile from earlier came back, though the sun was almost gone. "You will start being able to do new things now, Amelia. It will still take time, but you have as much of that as you could ever wish for." He swallowed. "And then some. Are you ready to go?"

"Home?" Amelia asked, disappointed. That was just like him, to tempt her with exciting promises, only to check his watch and tell her she had to go back to the house. But it did make her think of another question. "Will the basement here have to be as cold as the one in your house?"

"No," he said, taking her hand. "I simply prefer it

that way. Now come; we are not going home, and we don't want to be late for dinner."

The table was set; the plates and glasses were empty. The candles flickered in their sconces, light caught by the silver knives and forks and spoons, their wax not yet beginning to melt. About half the chairs were filled, the others clearly still waiting for their occupants to arrive.

"Amelia!" cried Madame Roseline, jumping to her feet, silk skirts whispering across the stone floor. "How delightful to see you once more, my dear. You will be dining with us?"

Amelia nodded and stilled her head to let Madame Roseline kiss her cheek. It felt impolite to remind her that Amelia couldn't see their food. Besides, she was too busy looking at Madame Roseline with new eyes, squinting through the dim light. Madame Roseline didn't appear a day older than Horatio—if anything she seemed younger, bubbling with life—yet she must be. She had been the one to turn Horatio into one of them. Maybe, if she asked nicely, Madame Roseline would tell her what the world had been like when she was young, what it had been like when she'd become one of the shadow-people. Maybe, if she was *really* nice, Madame Roseline would take her there.

Felix stood next, taking Amelia's hand to shake it, raising it to kiss it instead. She giggled.

"You have taken the first step?" Madame Roseline asked Horatio.

"An hour past."

"Then this shall be a most exciting supper." Madame Roseline clapped. "Take your seat, Amelia," she said, pointing. "That one will always be yours now. You are not required to join us for every gathering, but rest assured you will always be most welcome. Horatio can bring you, or you may come alone."

Startled, Amelia did as she was told. Did that mean she didn't need Horatio's help anymore to go through the door? Did it mean she could go anywhere she wanted? Anywhen? She'd thought she'd felt something change on the hilltop, a flicker, a tingle, but she wasn't magic like the rest of them yet. Surely she'd feel it if she were.

A start was good enough for now. The last dinner she'd eaten had been with her silent, tired parents, a scowling Owen, a confused Matthew, a sticky Lavender. Here she was with the finest crystal and china, surrounded by magic people in elegant gowns and fine suits—Horatio's was the only one showing any signs of wear. Felix folded back the lace at his cuffs, and she remembered it tickling her chin as she sat at the prow of a pirate ship. She would be one of them.

The remaining seats began to fill. Klaus, the one with the calendar castle, bustled in, waving at everyone, beaming at Amelia. Felix, spotting her confusion at the next arrivals, kindly whispered their names in her ear.

When the table couldn't hold one more person, Madame Roseline tapped her knife against her glass, the crystal ringing like a bell. "Welcome, everyone," she began. "We all know why we gather here, but as we have Amelia with us once again, and Horatio has just taken the first step toward her transformation, I feel it is a good idea to remind ourselves. There is no one quite like us, and almost no humans—Amelia excepted, naturally, at least for the moment—who know we exist. We are forgotten by those families we leave behind, the friends and neighbors who cease being able to recall that once there was a young girl or boy who lived in the house on the next corner or the next hill. Thus, it is our job to remember one another, to be one happy family, however far apart we may live, however widespread our precious calendar houses. Not to mention, of course, that these delightful soirees offer us the chance to sample new dishes we might not otherwise get to savor. With that, I wish us all bon appétit!" Madame Roseline clapped her hands again, but this time the sharp sound had the unmistakable tone of command. The door opened and two figures entered, silver trays hoisted on their shoulders.

"Who are they?" Amelia whispered.

"They are . . . like you, a few years from now," Felix replied. "More of Madame Roseline's."

"Will I have to serve dinner to everyone?"

Felix smiled. "No. She can be very strict when she wants to be."

"Was she strict with Horatio?"

"Um." Felix's eyebrows rose, as if he was surprised she knew this. "I do not know. That was, if you'll pardon the phrase, before my time."

One of the figures, a girl, placed a small silver cup with a lid on top of Amelia's china plate. Madame Roseline informed the table that Ivan—a bald, portly gentleman at the other end of the table—had brought their first course. Klaus had brought the wine with which the other server, a boy, was filling their glasses. Amelia wondered if she should pretend to eat for the sake of politeness, and whether she could ask for some apple juice. She was far too young for wine.

On either side of her, Horatio and Felix removed

the lids from their cups, and the most tantalizing scent wafted into Amelia's nostrils. It was Christmas dinner, or, no, chicken and mushroom pie, or possibly bread, fresh from the oven. Or pancakes. Shaking, desperate not to be disappointed, Amelia lifted her lid and set it down on the thick linen tablecloth.

The food inside wasn't any of the things she'd smelled, but there was *something* inside. A swirling mass of oranges and purples, liquid as soup and thin as air, that pulsed with a faint light. Everyone was using spoons. Amelia picked hers up, the silver clinking against the side of the cup as her hand trembled. Horatio had said she would be able to do things she hadn't been able to before. The tingle returned to her fingertips once more; she nearly dropped the spoon.

It tasted . . . of all the things she'd thought of, all her favorite things. Each mouthful was something different, new, delicious. The best food she'd ever eaten, and she wanted more, more. Warmth spread from her tummy to her toes and up to her head, which filled with strange pictures. A day out at an amusement park. Her stomach flipped from the roller coasters; candy floss melted on her tongue. She always loved going to amusement parks.

"What is this?" she asked. Horatio was deep in

conversation with the woman on his other side, but Felix leaned closer. "It is our food," he said, swallowing another spoonful.

Well, yes. She was clever enough to have figured out that much. "It makes me see things," she persisted.

Horatio whipped his head to face her, a wide smile stretching his lips. "What do you see?"

"A Ferris wheel," she said.

"Well done, my dear." He raised his glass and took a long gulp. "It's working."

"I'm supposed to see things?"

"Oh yes," he said. "Oh, yes."

The empty cups were taken away, replaced by plates of more odd, swirling stuff, this time in blues and greens. Felix picked up his fork, and Amelia couldn't see how she'd be able to pick any of it up with a fork; it would slide right off. Still, she copied him; she didn't want Madame Roseline or Horatio to think she was doing any of it wrong.

Bitterness exploded on her taste buds, like when her parents made her eat liver or spinach or brussels sprouts. A thunderstorm crashed through her mind, a roll of fear shuddering through her body and raising the hairs on her arms every time thunder cracked the sky. Amelia pushed her plate away, the food barely touched, but Madame Roseline smacked her lips.

"Delicious," she said. "Thank you, Simone. Goodness, children really do give us the best ones, don't they? So full of color and flavor. Outstanding."

Amelia coughed. She hadn't asked for some juice, and her throat was dry. What had Madame Roseline just said? The room was full of voices, laughter, the clink of cutlery on plates. She must have misheard. When everyone but Amelia had cleared their plates of every last speck of the stuff, these, too, were cleared away, and in their place the boy and girl put down wide glass goblets, glowing pink.

"Finally, dessert," said Madame Roseline. "Courtesy of dear Horatio. Enjoy, everyone."

Amelia walked through a house in her head, strange yet vaguely familiar. She stepped off the bottom stair and turned, following the sound of people. The people were in a dining room, much less elegant than the one Amelia actually sat in, though it had an air of *home* this one lacked. She stopped in the shadows of the doorway, listening, eavesdropping. "You didn't have to cook," said the man kindly; "I would have. You should be resting." Amelia could not see his face.

"Plenty of time for you to cook once this one's born," said a woman. Irritation flared across Amelia's skin, and footsteps hammered down the stairs; a boy appeared at the bottom. The part of Amelia's brain that knew where she was *did* drop her spoon this time. He was still recognizable, though he was younger than she was used to.

Matthew.

CHAPTER FOURTEEN

Memories

FRESH AIR HIT AMELIA'S LUNGS. The lawn shimmered by the light of gas lamps along the path. "I don't understand," she said.

"It isn't easy to, in the beginning," answered Horatio. "Tell me, first, did you enjoy the food? How did it taste?"

"The first one was the best thing I'd ever eaten, but—"

"There will be more of that in your future, an endless future. You will get hungry, and you will eat, and nothing else will ever satisfy you so much again. This is your food now, Amelia; this is what you must do to live. You are the lion who eats the antelope."

"I still don't understand." He wouldn't think she was so very clever anymore, but that didn't matter right now. She needed to know. Needed him to tell her.

"Memories, my dear Amelia, are how humans measure time. Oh, you may think it is watches and clocks, sundials and phases of the moon, but that isn't so, though all of those things have their place. If you had no memories, you would have nothing, no concept that any time had passed at all. It is because you remember the growing number of candles on your birthday cakes, because you remember a new first day of school every year, that you are aware of the great passage of time, the swing and cycle of it. Human memories give us time to spend in Victorian London, or on pirate ships. An hour here, an hour there."

"I thought it was the house that did that."

Horatio neared her, placed his hand on her shoulder. Nocturnal birds twittered in the trees. The moon hid behind a cloud, afraid to show its face. The air was weighted with magic, importance, detail. "It is that, too. You have a hearth in your bedroom at Nudiustertian House."

Well, now she knew how to pronounce it. "Yes," she said, confused.

"Think of the entire house as a hearth. Cold and

empty at first. You must place wood in the grate, as you must place people in the house. But even then, that is not enough. Memories are the match."

"But why do we have to light the fire at all?"

"Because without the fire, there is no life. Life is warmth; life needs warmth. We must light it, and we must keep it burning. Remember how delicious the food was, Amelia; just think about that. Think about what you will be able to do, all the places and times you will be able to visit. I'll take you back now; tomorrow we shall have another adventure."

The twenty-fourth door bloomed to life before them, drawing itself in the air until it was solid as a wall. Amelia stepped through, into the silence and dark of her uncle's office, his papers still strewn on the desk, his drawings of the house clipped to the angled table. He had known there was something strange about the house and was trying to uncover the mystery when he died. Sickness rolled through Amelia's stomach, mixing with the swirling memories there.

"You weren't the one who hurt them, were you?"

"Why would I have done that?" Horatio asked. "A tragic accident, that is all. But it brought you to me, and I'm sorry, but I see that as a magnificent thing. For many years I've been looking for someone to teach, to bring into our strange family. Go, Amelia. I shall return for you tomorrow."

"I—" she began, and stopped. He had returned to the shadows, gone. Amelia tiptoed out onto the landing and closed the door quietly behind her. Mum and Dad were downstairs, Lavender probably with them. Owen and Matthew were . . . somewhere. She read quietly in her room until Mum called her down for dinner, and she was quiet at the table, too. Mum suggested they all watch something on television together, but Amelia couldn't even have said what it was, she paid so little attention. The moment it was over, she said good night and climbed the stairs. In the bathroom she brushed her teeth and hair, washed her face. Freshly laundered pajamas were folded on the end of her bed.

That night she dreamed.

And in the morning she awoke ravenous, her growling stomach better than any alarm clock. The sun was barely up, and when she crept downstairs, the kitchen was empty. Noises are always impossibly loud in a quiet house; Amelia fetched a bowl, milk from the fridge, a box of cornflakes from the pantry, certain that any moment now her parents were going to come running to see what the earthquake was.

The cornflakes tasted worse than liver and spinach. Bitter, sour, the milk curdling on her tongue. She ate every last bite anyway and poured another bowl that didn't fill her up any more than the first.

Nauseated, dizzy, Amelia tottered back to the fridge. Maybe there was something better in there, something her stomach wanted more. Cartons of leftovers and the bowls of sliced fruit that were the reason for Lavender's constant stickiness turned her tummy over in a somersault.

Footsteps sounded on the stairs, and she remembered. It all felt like a dream, the supper last night, and she *had* dreamed. It wasn't Matthew coming down, as he had in the memory; it was Mum, with Lavender on her hip, Lavender's still-sleepy head on Mrs. Howling's shoulder. Mrs. Howling walked right past Amelia, opening a cupboard and pulling out a plastic cup with a red lid. She filled it with milk and set Lavender on the floor to drink it while she did complicated things to the coffee machine on the counter.

"Morning, Mum," said Amelia. A tin of coffee tumbled to the tiles, clanging through the house.

"Amelia! I didn't see you there! I'm sorry, darling. I'll put a light on." Coffee beans skittered as Mrs. Howling tripped to the light switch. The shadows disappeared. "I guess autumn's really here, huh? So dark in the mornings."

"Yes," said Amelia, not really listening. She was watching her mother's head. A swirl of green and yellow hovered around it. *Food,* whispered the house. *You are hungry, Amelia.*

Her fingertips went cold; the fire in the fireplace Horatio talked about had gone out. She needed it, that memory, but he hadn't told her how. The memory pulsed and glowed around Mum's head, its light growing stronger as Amelia stared. Drool ran down her chin. Mum was sweeping up the coffee beans with a dustpan and brush, oblivious to Amelia's roaring stomach.

Amelia opened her mouth. The swirl stretched through the air, and the scent filled the room. Not as delicious as the amusement park—duller, blander somehow. *Children give us the best ones,* Madame Roseline had said, but Amelia was too accustomed to ignoring Lavender, and there was no time to turn attention on her now. The memory swam across Amelia's tongue and down her greedy, gulping throat. Sweet, but with a hint of something like lemons, or salt. Images of Amelia's old house filled her head: a quiet morning, when Mrs. Howling had been able to sleep an extra hour. Mum missed their old house, their old life, too.

Amelia hadn't known that, but she knew now how her tummy stopped snarling, the warmth that wrapped around her as the memory did what the cornflakes couldn't. More. *More.* The huge house was full of people, and people were full of memories. Coffee beans clattered into the rubbish bin; Lavender gurgled around the spout of her plastic cup. The swirl around her head was one color, pale blue, its flavor simple as the crackers Amelia ate when she was ill. Lavender was too little, her memories undeveloped, uncomplicated. That was fine for a snack, but Amelia was still starving. Her father's would be like her mother's. *Children.* Owen and Matthew. All the noise had probably woken them up by now, and if it hadn't, well, Amelia was perfectly capable of making some more. Accidentally, of course.

The world whizzed past outside the car window. Amelia leaned against it, so stuffed she thought she might burst. Mum had seen the empty bowl on the table and thanked Amelia for getting her own breakfast. Which, technically, Amelia *had* done, but Mum had only noticed the bowl. She hadn't noticed the other thing Amelia had eaten in the kitchen.

Owen and Matthew had gotten ready for school,

and if they'd seen Amelia hovering, they hadn't seen fit to speak to her.

She was full of memories, and full of magic. Magic they couldn't do. School was pointless, a waste of time she wanted to use to travel. The end of the afternoon, when surely Horatio would come for her, felt very far away. Reluctant, she climbed out when they stopped in front of the school. Mum patted her head, told her not to worry about what had happened the other day. It would all be forgotten, just . . . save the stories for another time.

For the second day in a row, Amelia sat in the back of the classroom and didn't raise her hand even once. In front of her, Owen was leaning forward, eager to pay attention and catch up on the things he'd missed yesterday. Amelia passed the time by glaring at him, and several times he scratched the back of his neck, as if he could sense that he was being watched. By midmorning she was ravenous again, and she didn't understand. Horatio used the memories to travel through time, but she hadn't done that. If anything time had slowed down while Mrs. Murdoch droned on about long division. Paying no attention, Amelia thought instead about the supper, and the conversation after. Lions and antelopes. She needed the memories not only to travel, but to live.

Her stomach growled again. Nobody else seemed to hear it, but it drowned out the scratching of pencils and chalk, spread right to the corners of the room. Amelia blushed, sure that any second Mrs. Murdoch was going to turn from the board and ask who was making that ridiculous sound. Mum would be so angry if she got in trouble again.

Desperate, Amelia cast around, looking at her class-mates. Their heads were all normal, surrounded only by hair. Owen tapped his pencil against his textbook. Purple curled from his ears like smoke from a haystack.

Owen lived in the house. Apparently it didn't matter that they weren't there right now. He lived there, and so she could see.

She opened her mouth; the memory stretched across the distance between their desks. When she was younger, her teachers had given everyone a snack in the middle of the morning; this was no different from needing a glass of juice and a cookie. Owen was trying to remember how to do long division without writing all the numbers down, just because he thought he was so much cleverer than everyone else. Well, he wasn't. Amelia was the clever one, and Horatio had chosen her. She let the memory melt on her tongue like candy floss, felt it settle her stomach.

Math tasted better than she'd expected; she'd always been too busy with her dictionary to notice.

She ate one of Matthew's from across the lunchroom instead of the slimy macaroni and cheese the school always served on Wednesdays. Between English and history, she helped herself to another snack from Owen, glad, for once, that he was in her class.

"Good day?" Mum asked when she picked them up.

"Fine," said Amelia. She wanted to get home, tell Horatio all about her day, use all the time she'd eaten to go somewhere more interesting than school. Mum, however, had other plans. She stopped Amelia at the bottom of the stairs as the television burst to life in the next room, Matthew watching afternoon cartoons.

"Amie? Where did you say you'd put those pictures? I can't remember."

"In the attic," said Amelia impatiently, a thought sliding to the front of her brain. "Would you like me to go and find them?" No one would disturb her up there, and Horatio had found her there before. No time would pass while they were gone, so she could find the pictures and bring them back after she was done adventuring.

"That would be very kind, sweetheart. I'll tell you

what, you go do that, and I'll go start making pizza for dinner. You love pizza."

She did. She *had.* Now the idea of tomato sauce and gooey cheese stung the back of her throat as if someone were trying to poison her with just a thought. "Thanks, Mum," she said, hoisting a smile onto her face. *Hoist* was a good word. It spoke of things that weren't easy.

Burning leaves, and autumn light through the oddly shaped window. She would have a window like that in her calendar house, she decided. It was round, like a porthole, but with points all round the outside, like a child's drawing of a sun. The sun, like the trees it shone upon outside, measured time, measured the year.

Perhaps the most complete calendar house ever constructed. Amelia straightened her back and decided right then, right there, hers would be even better. She would think of things Horatio hadn't even considered, and he would brag about her to everyone at the elegant supper table, telling them how special and clever she was.

The boxes of photographs she'd lugged all the way from the wintry basement were exactly where she'd dropped them, tucked into one corner. Amelia opened the top of the first one, saw the damaged pictures, a pile of gray. One by one she pulled them out and piled them on the floor beside her, her knees aching as she kneeled. Halfway down, the slippery paper showed figures, smiles. The people she'd seen in Owen's memory: her aunt pregnant with Lavender, her uncle happy, his arm around her. Owen and Matthew stood in front of them. She'd never paid much attention before, when they'd visited at Christmas or over the summer holidays; there'd been no reason to. Now she could see that Owen looked a lot like Aunt Marie, and Uncle Hugo looked a bit like Mum.

Her stomach growled. The colors in the photograph began to swirl. A glob of drool splattered on Matthew's face.

Before she could think, Amelia's mouth was open and she was drinking, gulping, sucking down every last speck until only cloudy grayness was left. And it was like someone had put a bowl of chips in front of her, this box full of pictures. No one could eat just one chip. Again and again and again, she reached into the box until she'd finished the very last one and her stomach was as full as if she'd eaten an entire pizza by herself.

Only then, only then did she stop, and the real world gathered itself back around her. The pictures had been stuffed away in boxes, in cellars and attics, where no one would notice them.

But there were others in the house. Jumping up, Amelia ran down the stairs and across the landing to her room. Jumpers and T-shirts hit the floor as she dug in the drawer, hands scrabbling for the edge of a silver frame. The picture, when she found it, was as gray as its surroundings.

Horatio had eaten it. He'd eaten the ones in the attic, too.

"Clever girl," he said, stepping out from behind the curtain.

"I thought . . . ," she began, swallowing tears that tasted of a trip to the seaside. "Fix them! Put them back!"

"I cannot. Neither can you."

"But I thought we were just . . . borrowing them, the memories. Using them. You destroyed them, didn't you?"

"*We* destroyed them," he corrected her. "You have traveled on my time, Amelia, on my fire, if you remember what I told you about the hearth. I have had to eat twice as much in order to take you with me, so you see, you were using them too."

Amelia shook her head, trying to rid it of thoughts of horses and pirate ships. That was why he had taken her on the pirate ship, to show her that what they did was right because of who they were. Teaching her without telling her.

"All right, here is another way to think of it. You are occasionally given money, yes? So you may buy things?"

"I get pocket money," said Amelia. "I usually spend it on books."

"Well, then. Your parents give you the money, and they do not have it anymore; you do. Then you spend it; you give it to another. After that, you do not have the money anymore, but you have the thing that you purchased, correct?"

"Yes . . ."

"Humans who live in our houses give us their memories, and they do not have them anymore. They give us their *time*. And we spend it, going to all the marvelous places you and I have visited, just as if, instead of buying a book, you spent your pocket money on a trip to the zoo. You buy the experience. That is why it doesn't matter what the memory is of, any more than it matters what the money is made of. It is simply a measurement of time."

She *thought* she understood, as much as anyone could understand such a thing. "Why do we have to spend the money?"

"Because that is its purpose. Money is meant to be spent, and time is meant to be spent."

But it wasn't right. "Their parents are dead!" she said. "Memories are all they have left of them."

"Indeed," said Horatio, his usual smile on his face, the usual twinkle in his eye. Usual, except when he was tired. Weak and hungry because he'd been taking her on the adventures too. "And trust me, they have been living in their memories for some months now. It has been a feast. Do you not think it is a kindness, to remove such painful memories? Have you not noticed that they have been growing happier each day because they do not remember the things that make them sad?"

A flicker of doubt waved in Amelia's chest. Was it a nice thing to do? But she was suddenly, absolutely sure of something else. "You did hurt them," she said. It wasn't a question. He had lied. "You made something happen to my aunt and uncle. And you ate so many of Owen's memories Mum took him to the doctor."

Horatio spread his hands. "I had no choice."

"Why not?" The chalk marking caught her eye. "Uncle Hugo was studying the house. Was he about to find you?"

Horatio laughed. "No. He was simply interested in

its architecture. Flattering, of course, but no danger to me."

"Then *why*?"

"Because I had seen you in my future, Amelia, and I had seen you in their memories."

A thundering silence fell, hammering at the inside of Amelia's head. She had visited her cousins at their old house; they had visited her at hers. Sometime after they'd moved here, one of them had thought of her, and Horatio had gobbled that thought right up. She didn't want to know where he'd traveled on that memory.

"For nearly a hundred years I waited, knowing you would become my apprentice, my family," said Horatio. "Clearly, in the beginning I knew it would be a long wait, by your clothes and hair and the car you arrived in. But I was patient; I knew you would turn up. It was not in the way I expected, but here you are. And not only did the accident bring you here; it caused your cousins—the boys, at least—to live in their memories because they didn't enjoy their present. A feast, as I say."

"I don't want this anymore," Amelia gasped. "Turn me back. Make me normal."

A curious mix of surprise and desperate sadness took over Horatio's expression. "I can't do that, Amelia. We cannot change the future I've seen, and even if we could, you placed the first brick. The transformation has started. You will be the first family I will have other than Madame Roseline."

"But you *did* change something. You must have. You said we couldn't touch things, change things, bring anything back with us, but you must've done something to hurt Uncle Hugo and Aunt Marie."

"Only what was within my power to do. I destroyed most of the memories your uncle had of operating a car. A simple, elegant solution. Humans are remarkably resilient and remarkably stubborn. He could not admit that he couldn't remember, and so he convinced himself he *did* remember. Combine that with a storm, and . . . I told you, Amelia, that such memories can be deadly."

"I have no choice," whispered Amelia. "I never had a choice. You did all of this for me. You took me on the pirate ship to show me that what I would become was all right."

"Remember the fun we've had, my dear. That fun will be never-ending. Our human families forget us; we must create our own. I was changed too young to have a daughter, and I have waited since that moment to find the right one. You, Amelia. You are the special one."

"They'll forget me . . . because you'll eat all the memories they have of me."

"Clever girl," said Horatio again, and Amelia didn't want to be clever anymore. She wanted to be as dumb as a . . . no, not a brick. As a something. The right word escaped her, and she felt too sick to try to catch it.

Amelia felt herself turn as green as a tree in spring. She was sick all over the rug. It was in precisely the same colors as the letters on her bedroom door, and not jolly at all.

CHAPTER FIFTEEN

The House Outside of Time

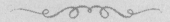

THAT NIGHT, AMELIA DIDN'T DREAM. In fact, she didn't sleep at all.

The tops of three hundred sixty-five trees glimmered in the moonlight. Her stomach complained, but she drew her knees up to her chest on the window seat and refused to move. No more.

Yes, more, said the house.

"Shut up," said Amelia.

She hadn't gone anywhere with Horatio; she never would again. He'd begged and pleaded and reminded her of lions and antelopes, but finally he had given up, told her he would return again tomorrow.

Well. Good for him. So what if she sat here getting

hungrier and hungrier. In the morning she'd tell Mum she was still ill and ask to stay home from school. Mum hadn't noticed Amelia had thrown up; Matthew had thrown a screaming tantrum about something, and Amelia had used the time to find a sponge. When she'd returned to her room with it, the strange, wispy stuff that wasn't like normal food had vanished from the carpet, and Horatio had tried to convince her to vanish with him. Instead, she'd told Mum she wasn't well and didn't want any pizza. Hiding out in her room, she couldn't hurt anyone, couldn't steal any more memories that were the only ones they'd ever have.

He should've told her from the beginning, but if he had, she would never have agreed, and now it was too late. As he'd said, her transformation had begun. What happened to shadow-people who refused to eat? Did they just fade more and more into the darkness until they were nothing at all?

She and Isabelle had solved problems before; she wished Isabelle were here now. Together she and Isabelle could find a way to bring all the memories back and turn Amelia into a human again.

Memories. Amelia had never really thought of them before, not the way she thought of books or breakfast. They were just a thing that happened, bringing a smile or a frown or a pang of homesickness. It had never occurred to her just how much people lived inside them, hiding. She had done it herself almost all the time since she'd moved here, thinking of her old house, her old teachers, her old best friend, who was busy making new friends. People lived in their memories and Horatio swallowed them up, each one worth a few minutes in whatever time he wanted to visit next. He'd even asked her for one, right to her face! But she hadn't known then what he was doing, that he needed the moments her memory would give him. That was why he carried the watch, she was sure of it. He knew how much he'd eaten, how much time he'd have to show her queens and cowboys.

And she couldn't, now, remember what that memory had been. It was a blank space in her mind.

She could break the watch, but he never so much as let her see it, never mind touch it. Besides, that felt too simple. Clocks and watches weren't important; he'd told her as much.

The house was important; she could break the house. Mum and Dad would probably notice that, though.

Her stomach roared again.

• • •

Mum let her stay home from school, believing Amelia was ill because Amelia could barely squeeze the words out through gritted teeth. Colors swirled around her head as she put a bucket next to Amelia's bed, just in case. She closed the door and Amelia opened her mouth, gulping clean, memory-free air. The pillow was cool against her cheek, and she dozed in fits and starts, too hungry to sleep properly, daydreams of elegant tables set with china and piled with food floating through her mind. When she opened her eyes, the bucket wasn't the only thing beside her bed.

It was a small package, wrapped in a scrap of lace. Amelia's fingers hesitated over it. She didn't trust him, trust that it was safe to touch.

You have no choice. You will become one of them, said a voice inside her head, and this time it wasn't Horatio's, but Amelia's own.

Her hand closed around the present.

The lace covered a long, thin box, and the lid of the box opened with a snap. Inside, on a cushion of deepest blue velvet, was a silver necklace set with a large, round amber stone just like the ones Horatio wore in a ring and Madame Roseline in her earrings. She had never looked closely at them, but surely suspended within them would be insects of some kind, as there was inside this one. Its legs stretched nearly to the edge of the stone, its wings spread in permanent flight. Frozen in time, forever. Just like Horatio and the others. Just like she would be.

Frozen. Cold. The necklace itself was cold, the silver chilled in her hand.

Horatio liked cold things. He *was* a cold thing. Their travels were cold, and the first time she truly thought she'd sensed him, it had been in the basement. He'd even told her that the basement of her calendar house wouldn't have to be so cold; he only preferred his that way.

And his heart, that was definitely cold.

Amelia threw back the covers, the necklace still clutched in her hand. The stairs creaked. Mum was in the conservatory with Lavender, and their memories sang to her, called for her to come and have a little snack.

No. Quietly as she could, Amelia opened the basement door and sank, step by step, into winter. She didn't know what she was looking for, but beneath the consuming hunger that growled from her belly, this felt like the right place to be. The floor was cold as snow on her bare toes. She hadn't put on shoes or socks today; she wasn't going anywhere.

Old junk cast shadows on the walls. She looked for one in the shape of a man with wild hair, like trying to find objects in clouds. There wasn't one. Only rusting bicycle frames and rickety shelves holding tins of paint. On a shabby dresser sat a grubby pipe, a broken Christmas bauble, a single child's shoe, a spyglass, a square of purple silk.

And a dictionary. Not Amelia's dictionary, but one she had seen before. The necklace fell from her hand with a clatter.

Another lie, then. He had told her they couldn't bring objects back, exactly like he'd lied about not hurting Uncle Hugo and Aunt Marie. Anger bubbled up within Amelia, mixed with a curiosity as ravenous as her hunger. The dictionary was frozen in time by the cold of the basement, exactly as it had been in the marketplace more than a hundred years earlier.

The leather felt exactly the same under her fingertips, and the moment she touched it, a memory whooshed into her mind. *Her* memory, one she hadn't realized was gone. "Take me somewhere fun," she'd told Horatio, the first time they'd gone to the past. The silk and the spyglass were from their adventures too.

Amelia didn't know anyone who smoked a pipe. It was cold, of course, the bowl empty, and she didn't recognize any of the faces that burst into her mind. The furniture was different and so were the plants, but there was no question it was the conservatory of Nudiustertian House. A family in unfashionable clothes sat on the couches and chairs. Inside the memory Amelia raised the pipe to her lips with a gnarled, wrinkled hand and smiled.

The images changed again as she touched the shoe. Again the room—the kitchen, this time—was different yet familiar. Amelia held a pair of tiny hands, leaning over a small, dark-haired child taking its first wobbly steps.

The memories made Amelia's stomach snarl, and, for the briefest of moments, they made her sad, too. Horatio had no family of his own, only the other shadow-people, and so he kept these, like little treasures. Would she feel as hollow when she became one of them? Would she sit in the shadows of her own calendar house, watching others truly live around her, never really able to join in?

She reached for the last object, the Christmas bauble. This time she knew exactly where she was, every aspect of her surroundings completely familiar. There was her old house on its hill, and there was a Christmas tree, and there was a remote control car on the rug.

And there was Amelia. This was not her memory.

She looked around at the other faces, not seeing Owen. It was his memory, then. His eyes she watched from. Horatio hadn't taken her version of this memory; he'd taken Owen's. She *did* remember it, the missing details in her mind filled in by the contents of the bauble. It was right after the car had gotten stuck in the snow. They'd rescued it and gone inside, and Mum had made hot chocolate for everyone. Amelia had told Mum that having Owen around was fun, and she wished he could visit more often. Owen had heard her, and smiled.

Yes, she remembered, but it was not her memory. Owen had remembered it too, even though it had happened more than a year before he'd moved here. At some point since he came, he'd thought of Christmas with Amelia.

She thought she knew when. Owen had mentioned it the first time they'd had a proper conversation. So it couldn't be the memory Horatio had spoken of, the one in which he'd first seen her. People in this house had thought about her. Her family had thought about her.

Tears froze on her cheeks, and she dropped the bauble back on the dresser. She was halfway back to the stairs when something occurred to her: These memories were already gone, already stolen. The people they'd belonged to wouldn't miss them.

She opened her mouth. The memories stretched from their objects and into her greedy, swallowing mouth. Too hungry to even taste them, Amelia gobbled every last drop.

The objects trembled. The crack in the side of the bauble began to lengthen. The leather covering the dictionary started to split. Amelia gasped and watched as shoe and pipe, bauble and book, silk and spyglass crumbled bit by bit, until they were nothing but piles of glittering dust on the old wood.

Amelia thought. It was easier to think now, in the frigid air and with food in her belly. On the dresser in her bedroom she had a snow globe with a roller coaster inside, bought in an amusement-park gift shop. The roller coaster was the memory—take it and the water and the snow from inside the globe and all you had left was a broken thing, useless and empty.

The basement had kept Horatio's souvenirs frozen in time, and the memories had kept them whole. Because that was how memories worked, wasn't it? No matter how old you got, you stayed as young as you were at the time of whatever you were remembering, and it was the act of remembering itself that kept those recollections whole. Kept them alive.

Horatio was wrong. It was not a kindness to take her cousins' memories away, however sad they might be. It was the only way for Uncle Hugo and Aunt Marie to keep living.

This time she did climb the stairs. Her stomach was still growling, and she had more thinking to do. She thought she knew where she could get more memories that had already been stolen by someone else. The memories the other shadow-people brought could be eaten in the strange dining room, outside of time. Madame Roseline had told her she was welcome whenever she wished; she didn't need Horatio to take her there.

Her uncle's office was the same as it had ever been. How dare it, when everything else had changed? But the door was still there, the door to nowhere and everywhere set into the wall. Amelia closed her eyes, concentrated, snapped her fingers, though she wasn't actually sure what that did. It was what Horatio always did. She thought of a happy memory and turned the handle.

The lawn spread out before her, the wide, low building set against the sky. Both times she'd come before it had been evening; never had she seen it in daylight. It looked like anywhere; it looked like any*when*.

Slowly she walked up the path, alert to every noise. Gas lamps overhead sat unlit, their fires extinguished. She felt better now, fingertips tingling with magic as she gripped the doorknob. Hopefully there would be food inside, someone else's memories. Still wrong, but less wrong than stealing Owen's and Matthew's, perhaps.

Perhaps not. But she couldn't ignore her growling stomach anymore.

Along the hallway the doors that were usually closed now stood open. Amelia peered inside the first, crossing her fingers that it held shelves with jar upon jar of swirling memories, or a big pot of recollection soup bubbling on a stove. It was just a boring sitting room, though, with silk-covered armchairs and shelves of books. The next was a proper library, more books and tasseled lampshades. Then a bedroom, its bed neatly made.

Madame Roseline always seemed to be the one in charge, so Amelia had somehow assumed the dining room was in her house, but this couldn't be her house. She'd have something grand and fancy, not a little bungalow like Amelia's old house on its little hill. Truly, this must be simply a place outside of time, a place the shadow-people had built so they'd have somewhere to gather and eat and drink, swallowing down the food they stole.

The kitchen was empty, cold, untouched. Amelia had the distinct impression it was there only because houses should have kitchens, not because anyone actually cooked here.

An empty kitchen meant no food. She checked the fridge just in case memories had to be refrigerated, but the light didn't even come on when she opened the door.

Just the dining room left. She didn't imagine the rest of them had abandoned a feast for her to find. The door was open a crack; she pushed it farther. Tablecloths and china and silver were nowhere to be seen at the long table, but the room wasn't empty.

"Hello, Amelia," said Felix from his usual seat. "You were wondering, weren't you? And wandering, ha. You were wondering. It is my house."

"You? You live here?"

"If you can call it that." Felix laughed, but it wasn't a happy sound. He twirled an empty wineglass, which Amelia was sure actually was empty, since she could see the memories now. "Yes," he said, shaking himself. "I live here. Why have you come to visit, if you didn't know that? You're several days too early for supper, and if you're looking for Horatio, he left some time ago with Madame Roseline."

Amelia crept farther into the dining room; Felix seemed so fragile he might shatter if she moved too quickly. Slow steps had the added advantage of giving her time to think. That she was hungry seemed too simple an answer.

"Sit," he said, sensing her reluctance. She took a chair across from him, instead of her usual one beside. Shadows, the same velvet indigo as his coat, rimmed his eyes.

"I found out what we eat."

"Also what you eat, now."

"I don't want to!"

Felix's head jerked up; he blinked as if fully realizing for the first time that she was there. The shout bounced off the stone floors and empty sconces. "You're hungry," he said, "and you don't want to eat the memories in your house. Horatio's house."

Amelia nodded, stomach snarling as loud as her yell to prove she wasn't lying.

"Wait here."

Blue and pink, the memory swirled on the plate he returned with a moment later. A shining silver fork slipped from his lace cuff into her hand. Her mouth filled with spit.

"It's safe," he said. "You won't be hurting anyone, taking anything, if you eat it."

She was swallowing before he finished his sentence. Warmth spread through her, pictures invading her mind. A young hand reaching, taking Madame Roseline's. She looked no different, the same age as she did now, but everything else Amelia saw was old: a stone hut, a dented iron pot, a blank-eyed woman in the corner, staring at nothing as she babbled unintelligibly to herself. The picture changed, the same hand placing a stone in a patch of grass. Happiness swelled inside Amelia's chest, happiness and something else. Safety? Madame Roseline was saving whomever this memory belonged to.

The happiness lasted a moment before it was suffocated by a gray cloud of despair. Starving, Amelia kept eating, but the flavor had changed, leaving a foul taste on her tongue as she looked out onto a lawn split in half by a path lined with gas lamps.

She ate the last bite and gaped at Felix. "That was yours," she said.

"Yes, it was. Don't worry," he added quickly, seeing her face; "I am not sad to lose it. Indeed. I've been saving it in case it could one day help someone."

"You don't like what you—we—are either?" she asked. "That's why you don't wear anything with amber on it," she guessed.

"I didn't know you'd noticed. No. When I discovered the truth, I begged Madame Roseline to change me back, but she refused. Said it was too late. I refused to eat memories, starved myself to nearly nothing. She was . . . not pleased, did her utmost to change my mind. Eventually her fondness for me won out, and we came to an arrangement."

"What arrangement?"

Felix drummed his fingers on the table, making his empty glass quiver. "This house is not a calendar house," he said. "It's . . . something else. Something . . ."

"Outside of time," Amelia finished. Felix brightened.

"Yes. I live here, provide a place for everyone to meet for the dinner parties, eat only what they bring me. It's easier if I can't see their faces."

"Why did you come with us on the pirate ship?"

"Because Madame Roseline still seeks tiny punishments for my betrayal. I'm sorry. I did the best I could to make the outing enjoyable for you."

It had been enjoyable, mostly, but that was before Amelia had found out how it was achieved. The same sadness she'd felt at his memory filled her again. Was this what she would become? Would she live here with Felix, waiting for the other shadow-people to bring them scraps of swirling food?

She couldn't bear to ask how long he'd been here, if time even passed the same way in this place. However long it was, it was too long, time without end. Being one of them, building her house, would be better than that.

They fell into silence, which was probably how Felix spent most of his time. Hiding away, only coming out to see people at supper. Which was of course nothing at all like what Amelia had been doing for months, keeping herself from Mum and Dad and her cousins, turning up at the dinner table because Mum and Dad insisted on it.

And Horatio had used that. He thought that because she didn't know Owen, Matthew, and Lavender very well, and because she was angry with Mum and Dad for making her move in the first place, she'd be perfectly all right with eating their memories and then disappearing from their lives forever.

Well. She was *not* all right with it. Isabelle might not be here to help her come up with a plan, but Amelia could do it herself, alone if she had to. She was going to find a way to fix this, somehow. She had to.

"You said," she began, waiting for Felix to raise his head, "you said Madame Roseline couldn't turn you back because it was too late. Does that mean she would've been able to if you'd asked earlier?"

"Perhaps," answered Felix, turning his head. "I don't think she would have, however, no matter when I asked."

No. Horatio wouldn't either. "He thinks I'll change my mind."

"Will you?"

"He said I don't have a choice; he said he's seen my future. But he's lied to me about other things!"

"What, exactly?"

"He told me I couldn't bring anything back from the places we visited, but he did. He filled things with memories and kept them in the basement. I saw things he'd taken from our adventures. Only I broke them."

Unexpectedly, Felix smiled. "Well. He should not have done that. People notice when things go missing far more than they do when their memories disappear. Humans have odd ideas about what is valuable. Regardless, if they are destroyed now, it doesn't matter." He sighed. "It would be so nice to have company," he muttered. "Amelia, when did you first eat a memory?"

She drew her eyebrows in, thinking. "Two days ago, at supper here."

"And how many did you eat before you found out the truth?"

Amelia thought harder. There'd been Mum's and

Lavender's in the kitchen the next morning after the cornflakes had tasted terrible, a few each of Owen's and Matthew's when they were getting ready for school, a few more during the day, then all the photographs. More than she could count. "A lot," she said, "but I was sick on the carpet and they all came out again."

"Just mine, since you were sick?"

"And the ones Horatio kept in the basement."

He'd looked so sad since she arrived that his sudden, wide smile almost frightened her. "There may still be time," he said. "Not much of it, but some. You have placed the first stone?"

"It was a brick, but yes."

"All right." Felix was almost vibrating with enthusiasm. "Do you understand why Horatio chose you? Why he wanted to make you into one of us?"

Madame Roseline had said something at the last dinner, hadn't she? Something about remembering one another, and Horatio had said as much too, but Amelia didn't fully understand. "I'm not exactly sure," she said.

"We stop existing as humans—stop aging—when all humans who knew us as such have died. We continue on as . . . as what we are for as long as we remember one another, which is forever. It is why no matter how much I starved myself of memories, I couldn't die. You exist in a place in between right now."

"Both sides remember me," said Amelia.

"Yes. You can make a choice. Destroy your family's memories of you, or . . ."

He didn't need to finish. Amelia's eyes widened. "How?"

Felix stood and hurried around the table to drag Amelia from her chair. "Horatio kept saying how clever you are, and it's best if I don't have too many memories of this conversation for Madame Roseline to find. She will find some, but by then, hopefully, it will be too late. Amelia, when you were traveling with Horatio, did you ever notice that some things seemed out of place? Things that looked as if they should be from a storybook, not reality?"

"Yes!" said Amelia. "Only the odd thing here or there, but yes!"

"Then what I will tell you is this: My parents were wealthy aristocrats who kept me sheltered away in a house with few servants."

Amelia closed her eyes, thinking, remembering the memory. Her mouth dropped open. "You can't tell . . ."

"Not always."

"And false memories . . . ," Amelia breathed. She

clapped her hand over her mouth, saying nothing more that Madame Roseline might see.

"I'll take care of the others, their memories of you. You deal with Horatio. If he returns here, I'll keep him until exactly five o'clock by your human time. Go."

"What will happen to you?"

He looked sad again, just for a second. "A punishment of some kind, I expect. Do not worry; it won't be too bad. I've made my peace with what I am, Amelia, and it will forever be a comfort to know I have helped you."

"Thank you," Amelia said. "Thank you, Felix." She ran from the dining room, down the hall, out of the house, across the lawn. And she ran back through the twenty-fourth door.

She didn't care what Horatio said he'd seen in the future. She was going to change it.

CHAPTER SIXTEEN

False Memories

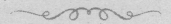

AMELIA GOT HER NOTEBOOK AND began to scribble a list. The house was quiet; Mum had left her alone, trusting her to behave herself. She'd listened to the car head down the long driveway, going to fetch Owen and Matthew from school. Mum shouldn't have trusted her, really, because Amelia had lied, saying she'd be carsick, when actually it was that she didn't think she could sit so close to Mum's and Lavender's heads, their swirling memories.

The list was of things she'd need. First on it was empty jars. Such things had a tendency to gather under sinks, with old dust cloths and tins of shoe polish and boxes of rat poison. Amelia almost smiled as she caught sight of the last. There was a lock on the cupboard, but it was only meant to keep Lavender out. She gathered up as many of the jars as she could, listening to them clink gently with every step she took back upstairs.

She'd need a rock, too, or a brick. Something heavy. It would've been quite poetic to use the one she'd placed on the top of the hill with Horatio, but she didn't know where it was, and she didn't have the memories to travel there even if she had, because she'd thrown them all up.

Another one would do, a very specific other one. *That* she'd get last. Horatio always seemed to know when something was afoot at his house. It had been dangerous enough, finding his treasures in the basement. He needed to stay away with Madame Roseline a little while longer.

And she'd need a book. She stood in her bedroom doorway for a moment, staring at the spot on the carpet where she'd been sick. It was invisible, not even the merest hint of a stain.

The squashy armchair waited for her in the library, the book she needed in the middle of a pile of others on the table. When she'd first been trying to figure out what was spooky about the house, it hadn't seemed to be any help, but she'd been wrong.

Right now Amelia felt as if she'd been wrong about a great many things. Ears peeled for the sound of the car returning, she flipped through the pages, looking for what she needed, a snippet of memory Horatio hadn't taken from her. In fact he'd left her well enough alone, once he'd revealed himself, just eating everyone else's memories instead.

Gravel crunched. A car door slammed. Amelia's mouth flooded with anticipation and spit. No. She must be strong. She wouldn't.

Not yet.

"Amie?"

"In the library, Mum," Amelia called, swallowing. The library door opened and Mrs. Howling peered in.

"Are you feeling better?"

Her heart thudded. She stared at the wall instead of the swirling around Mum's head. "I think I will be, soon," she said. "Where are Owen and Matthew?"

"They went to the sitting room," said Mrs. Howling. "They won't bother you in here."

"No," said Amelia. "I need them. I want"—she couldn't say what was really going on—"I want to play with them."

"Oh! Well, go ahead, if you're sure you're feeling up to it. And if you're going outside, wrap up. It's gotten chilly out there."

Outside. Yes, she would need to go outside, but first she had to get her cousins. It was never easy, admitting you'd been wrong, and Amelia had never had to do it much before. She took a deep breath.

They were sitting in front of the television. Amelia waited until she heard Mum in the kitchen, talking softly to Lavender. Her knees buckled as she saw their bright, pulsing memories leaking from their ears. Her stomach growled.

Not yet.

"I need your help," she said.

Owen sighed. He didn't look away from the screen. "I brought you your schoolwork. I'm not helping you do it, though."

"Like I need your help with schoolwork," Amelia shot back. She shook herself. "With something else."

"Why would we help you? You hate us."

"No, I don't," she said. But she had. She'd hated the house, and them, and then she'd loved the house and still hated them, and now she hated the house and . . . well, they were *her* family. Horatio didn't get to hurt them anymore. She wouldn't allow it. She'd been so mean, to Owen especially, pretending it didn't matter to her that he used to think about the times they'd played together in the snow.

"Hey!" said Matthew as Amelia stomped over and stood in front of the television, blocking whatever cartoon they were watching. "I don't hate you," she said again. "Please. I have a secret to tell you, and if I don't, if you don't help me, something *really, really awful* is going to happen. It's already happening."

"She's been reading ghost stories again," Owen said to Matthew, snickering. Amelia opened her mouth to argue and closed it again with a snap. Bad things happened when she opened her mouth too wide, and besides, that was exactly what she'd been doing before they got home.

"Please," she said through clenched teeth. "Come outside with me and I'll tell you everything."

Owen shrugged, but Matthew stood. Huffing, Owen followed, not wanting to miss out if Matthew was going to hear whatever Amelia had to say. They put on their coats and slipped out onto the porch. Amelia led them around the house and through the back garden, into the trees, deeper and deeper until they found the clearing where they had once played hide-and-seek. Yes, she had been trying to distract them then, to get them out of the house so she could go inside and talk to Horatio. Back when Horatio had been her secret. Back when she had been special.

Three hundred sixty-five trees surrounded them. Through their lacy branches, half their leaves covering the ground, Amelia could see the house. Sixty, thirty, twenty-four, seven, and all the other calendar numbers Horatio had managed to squeeze into its bricks and windows and stairs and fireplaces.

"The house is special," she began.

"You sound like Dad," said Owen, his voice half amused, half sad.

"Yes. And I think he knew, but he didn't know the real truth. He just thought it was a weird house, and it is, but it is so much more weird than he knew."

Amelia closed her eyes and turned away. They were full of memories now, both of them. She put her hand on her snarling stomach and took a deep breath of the mossy air. Time. It was time.

She told them about the house, its details, its purpose. She told them about Horatio, how charming he'd seemed at first, how exciting it had been to be the one he'd chosen. She told them about their adventures, the things she'd seen, resisting the urge to remind Owen of what had happened in Mrs. Murdoch's class.

She told them about discovering the truth.

"I don't believe you," said Matthew.

"Me neither," said Owen.

"All right. Think about why you don't dream here. You used to, didn't you, in your old house? It's so that you don't waste memories in dreams; your brain saves them all for when it's awake. Think about why you're forgetting things you should remember."

"But that's . . . that's normal," said Owen. "They told us that was normal. The doctor said it was. He said I was fine."

"It isn't," said Amelia. "Not like this."

Owen paced around the clearing. Amelia kept having to turn so she wasn't looking at him or Matthew. It was too much. She was too hungry. Felix had said she only had a little time; she'd already used up hours of it finding what she needed to find, waiting for Owen and Matthew to come home. They needed to believe her.

"If it's true," said Matthew, "you were eating our memories too."

Owen wheeled around. Amelia couldn't look away fast enough to escape the rage on his face. "Yeah!" he said. "You're the reason we've been forgetting Mum and Dad too!"

"I'm sorry," said Amelia. "I didn't know. I promise you: I didn't know. You can help me fix it, at least as much as it's possible for it to be fixed. And you *should* because . . . because we're family. We don't always have to like each other, but no one else gets to hurt us."

The mossy air stilled. It had a bite that promised winter. Leaves crunched under Amelia's feet as she struggled to stay on them, weak with hunger. This was it. They could choose to help her or they could choose to send her to be one of the shadow-people forever. If they refused, she would have no choice but to find something to eat, to call Horatio and tell him to take her away. They could choose to hurt her just as much as she had hurt them. They could choose to forget her as much as she'd tried to forget they existed, hiding away in corners of the house, refusing to play with or speak to them.

"What do we do?" asked Matthew.

Amelia exhaled. "Somewhere, there's a stone," she said. "It won't look like any of the other bricks in the house. It will be very, very old."

It was heavy in her hands, as heavy as the heart in her chest or her legs as she dragged herself across the attic floor. Or the words she forced from her throat. "Think of any memories you can," she said. "Memories you don't mind losing; it doesn't matter what they are. Horatio and his friends don't really care about that. Think of them and make them *as disgusting as you can.* Change them. Make them . . . not real."

"I don't get it," said Owen. "Why will that work?"

"I don't know if it will, but Felix—one of the others—hinted that it might. He said they can't always tell when memories are real or fake, and I've read about false memories. Yes," she said, sticking her tongue out at him, "in a book of ghost stories. I think it's like . . . You know when you eat too much candy floss at the fair, and it makes you sick, or if you have milk that's gone bad? It's food, but it's not really food. It's not good for you."

"So it's like poison?"

Amelia remembered the box of rat poison beneath the sink. "Yes," she said. "Exactly like that. Come on. Hurry. Make them mostly real, but . . . twist them. However you want." She placed the stone gently on the floor at her feet. Old as it was, it would crumble to dust if she dropped it.

Colors like fireworks began to explode from their heads. She was *so hungry*. Drool poured from her mouth and soaked the front of her shirt. Turning the first empty jar in her hands, she opened her mouth.

It was like being given an enormous chocolate cake for your birthday and not being allowed to eat a single bite. The memory stretched from Owen's head, smoky black with streaks of red, and she caught it, trapped it in the jar, and screwed the lid on tight. "More!" she said. "More! And hurry!" They had pried the stone free from the archway above the front door and run all the way up to the attic, feet thundering on the precisely numbered stairs, but Horatio was going to know soon that something was very wrong with Nudiustertian House.

That it was broken. If he didn't already.

One by one Amelia caught all the memories Owen and Matthew could make, until the late-afternoon sun shining through the oddly shaped window made the jars on the floor glow like a string of Christmas lights. It had been Christmas when he'd taken her to her old house to see the new family living there. Rage bubbled inside Amelia, quelling some of her hunger.

"All right," she said. Her wristwatch was nothing like Horatio's fancy gold one, but it was exactly what she needed right now. Two minutes to five. Horatio and Madame Roseline and the rest of them were right; time meant everything. She watched the hands tick. "Go downstairs," she told Owen and Matthew.

"No way," said Owen. "We want to see this."

Amelia frowned. Horatio would know they were in the attic, but perhaps that wouldn't matter. And if it all went wrong, they should see it. Someone should remember what had happened to her.

"Hide behind the boxes," she said. He'd still know; she'd just have to distract him before he could do anything about it.

The jars waited, a buffet of recollection. Amelia took a deep breath.

"Amelia," said Horatio, stepping from the shadows. How long had he been there? He was smiling, but his eyes glittered darkly. "There is something wrong. I can feel it. . . . What is it?" He asked the latter of himself, not her, a mutter under his breath.

"Nothing's wrong. Look!" she said, pointing at the floor beneath the window. "I got you a present, like the ones you've been leaving me."

He looked around the attic in the fading light, then at the memories.

"I'm sorry," she said. "I just needed some time to get used to the whole idea. I'm ready now."

He brought his hands together at his chest, smile widening. "Oh, Amelia, I am so very pleased to hear that. Madame Roseline will be too. I was slightly concerned, you know. Clever girl, figuring out how to catch them without eating them yourself."

"I know," she said. "Eat up, and we'll have an adventure."

The memory scented the air as he removed the lid

from the first jar, nose twitching. He drank it in a single gulp. "Now the next one," she said. It took him two gulps to drink the second. His eyes began to bulge, but Amelia understood the hunger, the thirst, how difficult it was to stop. Owen and Matthew hid behind the photographs she'd destroyed, one after another after another. She didn't need to encourage him to drink the next, or the one beside it, glowing and swirling all the colors of the rainbow mixed in with inky black.

But it didn't seem to be working. All hope was lost if it didn't work. It *had* to work. Horatio set down the last empty jar. As he stared at her, his face began to change. She had always seen him mostly cheerful, occasionally tempered by the tiredness of taking her adventuring on the time he'd gathered. Now his mouth twisted; his eyes snapped dangerously; his long-fingered hands clutched his stomach.

"You—" he said. "What have you done?"

"Aren't they any good?" she asked. "I tried to get good ones."

Horatio fell to his knees, retching, memories spewing from his mouth, their sickly smell mixing with the attic's aroma of burned leaves. They swirled away into nothing as he kept vomiting, everything, every memory he'd eaten for days.

Amelia swallowed hard. This was the last part.

"I'm sorry!" she said, rushing to him. She filled her head with every memory she had of Horatio, from his first appearance to the pirate ship to him drinking from the jars just a moment ago. She thought of her first days in the house, the oddities that struck her even before she knew what was causing them. "Here!" she said, knowing the colors were a cloud around her, boiling from her ears like steam from a kettle. "Drink mine! Mine are good!"

On his hands and knees he turned his head, mouth gaping at her. She watched the memories stretch, pour down his throat, felt her head empty of nearly every image of him. But she was hungry now, so hungry at their scent, so weak because she hadn't eaten in too long. It was unbearable being around them.

Hold on, whispered her own voice inside her head. *Hold on one more minute. Throw the rock.*

She fell to the floor, crawling for it. She couldn't. There was no strength inside her limbs. "Owen," she croaked, begging. "Owen, help me."

The boxes tumbled as Owen jumped up, racing for the stone. Horatio had seen it now too; his arm was reaching.

"You foul, evil, horrible children!" he yelled, the words scratchy and dark.

Details were important. The stone was important, and so was the last window Horatio had placed
in Nudiustertian House. Amelia knew him, knew he
would have saved that to be the final thing he did.
Number fifty-two, the sun-shaped window that let in
the day and the night, that kept the cycle and spin of
time turning through the house.

Owen reached it first, snatching it from Horatio's desperate clutches. He lifted it easily, and the stone soared
through the air, shattering the glass and tumbling out
into the falling night, down, down to the ground. It was
so old, the stone, so full of history and memory from the
house that came before it, the house it had been taken
from. It exploded into a billowing cloud of dust.

Horatio screamed. Amelia dragged herself to her
feet and lifted him, light as the shadow he was. The jag-
ged glass tore his dusty suit as she sent him out where
he belonged, to join the other snippets of darkness
that would disappear by morning.

Felix had said he'd take care of the others. None of
them would remember her. She would only remember this, getting rid of him. All her other memories of
their adventures were gone, a blank space in her mind.

"Amelia? Owen? Matthew? What on earth is going
on up here?"

Reality returned, brought by Mrs. Howling's voice. Amelia and her cousins stared at one another as Mum's footsteps climbed the stairs.

"I'm sorry, Mum," said Amelia, panting. "We were playing and . . ."

"And we broke the window," said Owen. "It was my fault. I'm sorry, Aunt Susan. I can pay for it from my pocket money."

Mrs. Howling brushed her hair from her forehead. "It's just a window," she said; "don't worry about that. Stay out of the attic while we get it fixed, though, all right? Are you ready for supper? Amie, how's your tummy; do you think you can eat?"

Amelia nodded. Yes. She wanted pancakes and lasagna and cornflakes and pizza. She wanted to kick Owen under the dinner table where Mum couldn't see, but she'd play with him after. She, Owen, and Matthew would keep their shared secret, telling only Lavender, when she was old enough to know. She smiled at both of them, and together they followed Mrs. Howling down the stairs, into the rest of the house.

It needed a new name. Amelia would look in her dictionary for one she could pronounce.

EPILOGUE

A SHADOW MOVED THROUGH THE night. Slowly, for it was weak, and it was hungry. The only reason it could move at all was the second shadow, sliding along behind it. She was angry, and disappointed, but she had been the one to create him, and she wouldn't desert him now. He hobbled on borrowed time, through the woods and up the hill. This act alone took nearly all his strength—she could give him more, if she hadn't decided to punish him for his failure. Madame Roseline could be very strict. She doled out memories to feed him as a mother starling would her chicks, keeping him only barely alive through what would be a long, cold, endless night.

The brick was where Amelia had left it. Horatio looked beseechingly at Madame Roseline, who shook her head. He must be the one to do it. She had refused him a piece of her house, forbade any of the others from offering him assistance. This brick was the last piece left, the final start of the magic. It would take time to rebuild, time in which he would remain weak and hungry.

Horatio hoisted the brick, almost letting it slip from his shaking fingers. He dragged it, and himself, a few feet to the left and dropped it with a blend of sheer relief and flickering anticipation. He had stood on this very spot and told Amelia about the turning of the year as they looked out upon the treetops.

There were different kinds of years, of cycles.

A new one was only just beginning.

Turn the page for a sneak peek at
Spindrift and the Orchid.

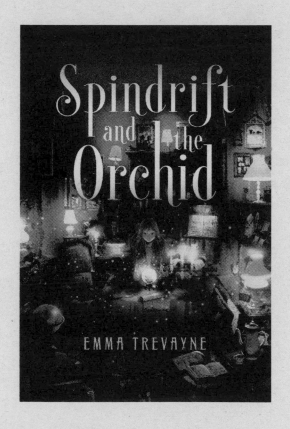

A Story Finally Told

IT STARTED, AS ALMOST EVERYTHING does, with a word, just like this story. *It*, you're wondering. What is *it*?

I'll tell you. I'll tell you everything, for when you have kept a secret as long as I, the only proper choice after deciding to unburden oneself is to tell all of it, from the first word to the last one. I can say right now that the last word is *rain*, but that won't do you much good without all the ones before it, so I'll share those, too, in the right order. I have stayed silent this long and could do so for whatever time I have left to me. I've stayed silent out of respect, yes, and out of fear as well, if I'm honest. The time comes, however, when one must stop being afraid.

Should someone read this and choose to seek out the mystery for themselves, the consequences of that decision are theirs alone and do not rest on my aging shoulders.

Where was I? Oh, yes. Words. Words don't frighten me anymore, though perhaps they should. There are some things about some words I must tell you before we begin.

Any dictionary worth reading will tell you that "spindrift" is a mist over an ocean, spray thrown up to the skies by a gale's crashing waves. I've seen it with my own eyes, felt its chill on my skin, slipped on it across the decks of a great and beautiful ship pitching in a storm.

But.

"Spindrift" is something else, too. Some*one* else. She is a girl, of dark hair and seawater-blue eyes and skin as pale as whitecaps. A girl who thought she was ordinary.

And the orchid is not only a precious, blooming flower. It is a curse.

—*M.D.*

17th day of the Month of Souls, in the Year of the Forgiven
N 48°51'24", E 2°21'03"

The Customer

THE LANE WANDERED SLOWLY, TURNING This way and that as if to look in the shop windows at the work being done by the artists and artificers within, or peer through the glass of *the* hothouses at the rare, vivid blooms. From a distance came the sounds of the river, its waters churned by merchant ships bringing silks and spices, oysters and pearls, and of course, orchids, the latter the most prized bounty of all.

At the end of the lane, where the doorframe rotted gently and the cobblestones slipped underfoot, a shop waited for customers.

It never had to wait long, though this was not the kind of place people wandered into by accident. Its proprietor could easily have afforded one of the large, gilded properties on Magothire Street, where even the trees were leaved in gold and silver, but he preferred to stay. Those who needed him—and that number included a wide swathe of the city's alchemists, inventors, nobility—knew how to find him while maintaining their privacy. One kept out so many undesirable customers by being difficult to find.

The girl sitting at the shop's counter thought, personally, that it got any number of strange customers, but her grandfather seemed to think they were the right kind of strange.

Her elbows made marks on the polished wood in front of the book she was supposed to be reading. Instead, she daydreamed of an ocean she couldn't quite remember, salt and spray and fin. Like the scales of a fish, they flashed in and out of sight too quickly to catch. If she closed her eyes and tried, truly tried, she couldn't recall anything at all. It was only when she was doing something else that the air would briefly, suddenly tinge with the scent of seawater.

Grandfather had forgotten, in that way of his, that there was no school today. He often forgot to put shoes on, too, shuffling around in a pair of threadbare slippers, or to turn on the lamps when the sky outside began to darken.

The absentmindedness didn't worry her, though,

because it came from his brain being full to bursting with other things. A customer could come in and ask for a set of clairvoyant wind chimes (which would always play the music the owner was thinking of at that particular moment) or binoculars for looking at a specific moment of the past or a book that wrote itself page by page as the reader watched. Grandfather would knit his bushy eyebrows together for an instant before unearthing the very thing from the dimmest recesses of the farthest shelf. If the shop didn't have what the customer was looking for, Grandfather would get a faraway look in his eye as he remembered exactly when he'd last sold such a thing.

Spindrift didn't know the contents of the shop nearly so well. Oh, she was good enough at the things in the cabinets that lined the walls of the front room and in the glass display cases set into the wooden counter, but she didn't understand the objects the way Grandfather did. To her, they were simply wood and metal and crystal and cloth, whereas to Grandfather they seemed almost alive.

So it was a good thing that when he left her alone to mind the shop, as he had done today, he always promised, just before he closed the door behind him, that he wouldn't be gone long. If someone came needing something complicated, she might not be able to help as well as he could.

In fact, she'd had only one customer, a grumpy old lady who complained a compass she'd purchased didn't work. It was supposed to point her in the direction of wherever she wanted to go, and yet it had taken her to her sister's home. Since they didn't speak, obviously the compass was quite broken. Spindrift suggested the woman come back to speak to Grandfather when he was here, but she was having none of it. Sighing, Spindrift opened a drawer behind the desk and traded the compass for a small pile of gold coins.

She went back to her book, which was interesting not because one of her teachers had assigned it—that could be hit or miss—but because the history of Lux, the city spread out around her, was fascinating to Spindrift since it wasn't her history. She had come here when she was young, after the accident. The sea was her home; she only lived here.

While she didn't know the shop as well as Grandfather, she knew the sound of the door creaking open as well as her own voice. Some customers barged in, certain of themselves and certain they were ready to part with a whole handful of weighty gold coins for one (or several) of the treasures here. Others tiptoed, perhaps deciding that they were here merely to look, not purchase. Invariably, however, Grandfather found something that took their fancy so thoroughly they simply had to have it, right this minute.

This customer was somewhere in the middle. He stepped inside, but kept one arm out straight and rigid to hold the door open, as if he might dart out of it again without a word. His clothing was too heavy for summer, a thick black brocade, the coat buttoned all the way to the neck.

"Good morning," said Spindrift politely. Grandfather wouldn't be pleased if he thought she'd chased anyone off with rudeness.

The man's thin eyebrows rose. They were as black as his clothing, and his hair, too. He hesitated, quite clearly waiting for someone older and more responsible to step out from behind a curtain to serve him. Not this short, thin thing of a girl, halfway through a child's schoolbook.

A chillier wind than Spindrift expected blew through the open door and rustled the book's pages. So perhaps he needed the heavy coat, after all. "May I help you?" she asked.

He tilted his head to one side, which made his long hair brush his shoulder. "Possibly," he said after a moment. "I am looking for something quite specific."

Spindrift swallowed. Exactly the kind of customer she'd been hoping not to get. Then again, perhaps his wish would be so specific that he'd know the thing he sought as soon as he laid eyes on it. "All right," she answered, marking her place in her book and hopping down from the high stool Grandfather kept at the counter for her. "What is it?"

"Well, it's . . . it's difficult to explain, you see."

This was not an unusual answer among Grandfather's clientele. "Go on," said Spindrift.

The man's hands—gloved, she noticed now—folded and writhed together. The door swung shut, but he made no move to step toward the cases and cabinets to look for his mysterious object. Instead his eyes followed every one of Spindrift's smallest movements as if she would abruptly leap over to a shelf and withdraw the thing he wanted without him having told her what it was.

"It . . . Well, it hardly matters. An unimportant trinket, I assure you. Simply a token I wanted as part of a collection."

"What sort of token?"

"A flower."

Now it was Spindrift's turn to raise her eyebrows. "A flower?" she repeated. There *were* flowers here on occasion. Elegant roses crafted in finest gleaming silver, whose thorns could be tipped with poison, or crystal lilies that would remain unchanged for years, decades, until they wilted on the day of their owner's death. Grandfather didn't have anything like that now, so far as she knew. This man would have to return when Grandfather was here.

"A black flower, one that blooms as you look at it," said the man. A strange, slow smile crept over his thin face. "Tell me, little girl, have you ever seen such a thing?"

Spindrift pictured her grandfather, the deep thought he entered as he remembered everything that had ever passed under his nose in this shop. She didn't have his memory for it, but she felt sure she'd remember something like what the man described. "No," she said, meeting the customer's eyes. "I'm sorry. I've never seen anything like that, but if it's a living flower you're after, you might try one of the hothouses. You passed a few on your way here, and there's larger ones on Magothire Street. I've seen ones that do special magic, especially the orchids. Maybe there's a kind that blooms in front of you; I know the hunters are always bringing new ones back."

The man's smile spread, reaching his obsidian eyes. "An orchid," he whispered. "Yes."

Grandfather returned a few hours later, which was an interesting interpretation of *I won't be long,* but he could be like that. Had been like that all Spindrift's life, or all of it she'd lived with him, which was nearly the same thing. There'd been no more customers after the slightly odd orchid seeker, who had left with his hands empty but his eyes still full of that strange smile. Spindrift told Grandfather about him because he always wanted to know who'd visited the shop in his absence, but he merely shrugged and took his place behind the counter, allowing Spindrift to return to her book. She was halfway through when the sun began to sink and her stomach began to rumble.

With the shop locked up tight, Spindrift and Grandfather climbed the stairs in the back to the home they shared above. Before she arrived as a baby, Grandfather had lived in just two of the rooms, a groove in the carpet worn between the one where he slept and the kitchen for his endless cups of tea. After she came, however, he had put furniture everywhere and set up a nice room for her, with a cot to keep her safe until she grew old enough for a proper bed.

She liked hearing stories about his life before she'd come to Lux, on the rare occasions she could persuade him to tell them. All too often he changed the subject to her schooling or what she might want for her birthday or when her two best friends, Max and Clémence, were next coming to dinner.

Now he went straight to the kitchen and suddenly started to move with the speed and dexterity of a man half his age. It might surprise some of his customers to learn that Ludovic Morel was one of the best chefs in all of Lux, at least as good as the cooks in the palace or the restaurants near it, where the waiters spoke in whispers and wore gloves so as not to smudge the silver spoons. Then again, perhaps it would surprise no one, given the attention he gave to the treasures he sold. Either way, Spindrift sometimes thought chickens would line up like customers for the privilege of being roasted by him. He stood at the counter, his back to her so she couldn't see what he was creating, but she was sure it would be something delicious. Her stomach growled again, even louder, and he laughed, a dry, old laugh that matched his stooped shoulders and white hair and, somehow, his threadbare slippers too.

"Patience, *chérie*," said Grandfather. "It won't be long, and worth the wait in any case. Have you finished your book?"

"Not yet, but I will."

"Good girl. Go wash your hands and prepare the table, please."

"Will we need spoons for dessert?" she asked hopefully, and he laughed again.

"Of course, my little Spindrift. Now, hurry."

She turned from the kitchen doorway and skipped through the apartment, making her feet thump as heavily as possible on the patches of wood between the rugs. There was no one in the shop below to disturb. Her fingers trailed over the fancy silk wallpapers. The pattern of raised flowers made her think of the customer and his orchid; she hoped he'd found what he was looking for at one of the hothouses. Moonlight streamed through the large windows and painted the surrounding rooftops silvery white. If she stood at the window in her bedroom and squinted, she would just see it glinting off the glass roofs of those same hothouses, the delicate plants within them well protected.

But Grandfather had told her to hurry. Quickly she washed her hands and dried them on her skirt, ignoring the perfectly clean and usable towel hanging from a hook.

She didn't know what had possessed her grandfather to put such a large table in the dining room when she came to live here; it had been just her, not a dozen hungry sailors.

Only Spindrift had survived, blown safely back to land as if she'd been light as mist. She was sure that wasn't the way it *really* happened, but since it had probably been terrifying and she couldn't remember it anyway, it did no harm to keep a nicer picture in her head. Also, it was why Grandfather called her Spindrift instead of her actual name, and she liked that.

She knew only bits and pieces of the real story because she'd been so young, and no one else who'd been there could tell her anything now. Grandfather had put together some of it from the people who'd found her and the note tucked into her blankets, wrapped in oiled leather to protect it from the water. But these things together didn't tell the whole tale. It was like when she and Grandfather used this table to assemble puzzles; she had a corner, a few strips of edge. Only when the last piece was in place would the picture begin to move, revealing truth and memory.

Unfortunately, most of the pieces were at the bottom of an ocean, never to be found and gathered together.

The dessert spoons clattered into place. Spindrift couldn't remember having set the rest of the table, but there everything was, knives and forks and spoons and thick linen napkins. Grandfather always sat at the head of the table and she always sat to his right. The ornate chandelier above was a relic from his shop, a rare artifact that had come into his hands and with which he'd been unable to part. Right now it was the moon, with tiny stars circling around it. At daybreak it would shift, become a sun that brightened with each passing morning hour. Below it, farther down the table, was a vase of roses, their buds still tightly furled. Spindrift stared at one for several seconds, willing it to bloom as she watched.

Nothing happened. Slightly disappointed, she took goblets from a cabinet in the corner to be filled with water and elderflowers for herself, wine for Grandfather. He must have heard the clink of crystal because he appeared with a tray covered by a silver dome. It was almost always just the two of them—and when they had guests it was only Clémence and Max—yet he served dinner every night as if it were the grandest of occasions.

"Your napkin," he said as he set down the tray. Spindrift unfolded it and put it across her lap.

"Thank you. Your mother would never forgive me if she thought I wasn't teaching you your manners," he said. His eyes twinkled and his tone was light, but Spindrift sat up straighter and gave him a sharp look. He didn't often mention her mother; he would always wait until Spindrift asked and then answer her questions—or tell her as much as he thought she should hear, which often wasn't the same thing. "She was always very tidy," he continued. "Though I don't suppose there were very many clean napkins on her ship."

"Why didn't you ever visit her on it?" Spindrift asked. "Surely she would have let you."

"Begged me," said Grandfather with a smile, "but I far prefer looking at the ocean to being bounced around upon it, thank you very much. And it so rarely came anywhere near Lux. Emilie was off sailing the world with your father, and soon enough with you as well, but she wrote me a letter each time she reached a port. I still have them, and it occurs to me . . ." Grandfather cleared his throat and removed the silver dome from the platter. So hungry before, Spindrift now paid no attention to the food. "Yes. I've been thinking it is perhaps time for me to share them with you."

Her stomach felt suddenly full, though she hadn't taken a bite, but full of something that wriggled and lurched. "Letters?" she asked, her mouth dry. "What sort of letters?"

"Oh, you know. News from the seas, from her adventures." He did not look at Spindrift as he said this, making a show of filling her plate and placing it before her.

"Why now?" It was a dangerous question; it might make Grandfather think twice about giving her the letters, but it was out of her mouth before she could stop it. Still, he didn't meet her eyes. Water splashed onto the table as he filled her goblet from a jug held in a shaking hand. Only when the water was at the brim did he set the jug down and raise his head.

"You are growing, little Spindrift, faster than I would like, perhaps. I am growing older, too, so perhaps it is a good thing you are turning into such a young lady, a person. And a person should know where they come from, or as much of that as is possible."

"Can we read them now?"

"After dinner, and I warn you there are more than we will get through in one evening. It will be a project for us, or if you prefer, you may read them on your own. I would understand."

"No," said Spindrift. "I don't think so. We'll do it together."

Finally, his smile returned. He patted her hand and picked up his fork. "First, food. Nothing worth doing can be done on an empty stomach. Bon appétit."